CONTENTS

LIGHTS, ACTION, CAMERA AND MURDER

VOL. 5

SHARON E. BUCK

SOUTHERN CHICK LIT

CHAPTER 1

The studio was dark, my brain was fried, and I was a lunatic.

What had I been thinking?! There were five, count them five, hormonally challenged, caffeine-and-sugar infused women in the television studio wreaking havoc on the producer, the director, the production manager, the floor manager, the camera operator, anyone within range of their voices. Not to mention the audio guys were probably going nuts trying to adjust the sound levels of these women on doing voiceovers for the show. They sounded like South American monkeys who had just been captured by warrior natives. Shrill screaming was an understatement.

I had a headache.

Maybe I should back up a moment and explain what was happening. You might want to sit down, kick off your shoes, and have your favorite beverage, or snack, at your fingertips. Yeah, it's going to take a moment or two and you should be comfortable before reading any further. Hey, I'm only thinking of your health and well-being.

I'm Parker Bell, I own a very successful cyber security company in Atlanta that does work for various government agencies. Stop yawning, it's really not that boring. Well, yeah, it can be. BUT, I have employees who do most of the work. I am also a best-selling crime author. That's a lot more fun.

I'm in my mid-thirties, I'm not telling you exactly how old I am because, really, who cares? I'm the average height of your average American female, five feet four inches. I have baby fine, light brown hair that refuses to conform to any type of hair styling.

Forget the blow dryer and curling iron, I don't have the patience for either one, and short of shellacking my hair into place for the next one hundred years, I either wash it and run my dainty little fingers through it to let it air-dry or I wash it and go to sleep on it. I make no apologies for just combing my hair and being done with it. Yep, that's my version of styling my hair.

My personal style is, well, what I consider as being computer geek stylish has been referred to as frumpy-dump. Yeah, whatever, and that person is no longer my friend.

Although I have now upgraded from jeans and tie-dye tee shirts, the decade of hippies, peace, and love appealed to my free spirit nature, to jeans and or-ange-and-blue Gator wear.

Basically, if my clothes can't be worn with sneakers or maybe leather sandals, it's probably not ever going to find its way into my closet.

Every once in a while, I do have to attend a meeting and I do own appropriate, professional business attire but I feel like an alien from Mars who's being tortured by the human constriction of clothes.

I am somewhat, cough cough, sarcastic although I do sorta, maybe, make a controlled effort not to be that way. Okay, so I'm lying. I find most of my remarks funny and make little to no effort to control anything that decides to slip out of my mouth and into the air.

Most of my friends don't consider that one of my more endearing qualities. The fact that they're still friends with me is somewhat amazing. However, they have learned never to ask me a question they don't want an answer to because I will answer any question that is asked of me.

I have brown eyes but not the kind that gets me out of speeding tickets with the police. They're just nice-looking brown eyes.

I am single and being single can be a plus, although it does get lonely at times. Those internet dating sites are not all they're cracked up to be. I can't find a man who can multi-task at one time - breathe, talk, and has a sense of humor - within five hundred miles. My assistant Missy says it's because I'm too picky. I prefer the word discerning.

Being transparent here, I do have one man who thinks I'm the goddess he's always wanted. It's Joe D. Savannah of We Make Money, CPAs. He was my first love boyfriend and is on wife number three. His version is he keeps marrying someone who he says is like me.

Let me point out, every one of his wives has been taller than me, has blonde hair, has a MUCH larger chest than I do and, you guessed it, they're nothing like me.

The only reason why we never married was because he wanted to be a big fish in a small pond and I thought I'd die in a small pond.

Anyway, back to the five hormonally challenged women in the studio.

They're the Lady Gatorettes - Misty Dawn, Myrtle Sue, Flo, Rhonda Jean, and Mary Jane – and they suddenly became very popular on their local radio show, then went national and then some very stupid, stupid person who thought he was a genius decided it would be great to have them on a reality TV show.

This had now turned into the TV show from h, e, double hockey sticks.

The girls were loose cannons at best and beyond crazy at their worst. Oh, did I mention that I'm also a newly inducted member? Yeah, I know, that doesn't say a whole lot about me either.

I became an honorary member after they had saved my life on a couple of occasions, and I had stood up for them on others. I am also an avid University of Florida football fan.

Did I mention they are RABID Gator football fans?

Several years ago, they had decided to join the local Gator booster club. Apparently, they may have been a wee bit too exuberant for the white-collar-and-tie group. There was an ugly rumor that the cops had to be called to escort them out of the meeting. Both sides did allow that there was way too much excitement in the room at the time, but the cops did not arrest anyone. As far as both groups were concerned whatever allegedly happened did not actually happen.

The girls were strongly encouraged not to come back. They were highly incensed and started calling themselves the Lady Gatorettes if for no other reason than to annoy the booster club members greatly.

It's time for you to meet them and maybe get a sense of their personalities. Warning, if you see any of them on the street somewhere, please do not have a doughnut or a cup of coffee in your hand. It could get ugly very quickly if you don't offer up these precious items as a sacrifice to the girls.

The Lady Gatorettes are fervent and beyond fanatical when it comes to the University of Florida's football team. As far as they are concerned, the Gators should be national football champions every year.

Keeping in line with that thought process, they mail, email, and overnight various football plays for the team to use as well as sending encouraging letters to the various members of the team.

Misty Dawn is the ringleader of the group and was so named because she was born on a foggy morning. Her mother, being the superstitious kind, took this as a naming sign and that's how Misty Dawn got her name.

While you might think she would be a soft, gentle person nothing could be further from the truth. She could make a sailor blush with her vocabulary and would have made the perfect Marine since she believed in being swift, silent, and deadly.

Let me be fair and say she's never said any horrendously bad words in front of me. Well, nothing that I haven't, maybe, personally used over the years. I just don't do it on a regular basis.

Misty Dawn's married to John Boy who works in construction. He's afraid of no one except his wife. He's learned over the years to let her vent when she needs to; otherwise, she goes on a killing rampage in the chicken house. The chickens try to hide in the hen house whenever she stomps out to their yard.

He apparently didn't let her vent enough one time, the key words being one time, and she went out to the chicken house and killed fifteen chickens. And, yes, they do live on a farm.

John Boy has said, away from Misty Dawn, he was so tired of eating chicken after fifteen days that he would let her talk all night if he had to and he wouldn't say a word. No more chicken dinners for him.

Misty Dawn has dark hair, brown eyes, and has that long, lean look of an athlete. She's not but since I look like a turtle in heat trying to run, I'm not challenging her to a foot race any time soon. She's outrun me on several occasions.

Flo is a tall, slim waitress who used to have long out-of-a-bottle blond hair but has now had it cut to a more manageable short bob. The blond part is still out-of-a-bottle she does herself. Although once she did have a customer complain that he had found a long strand of blond hair with a dark root in his food. The restaurant manager threatened to fire her. Flo was highly indignant and shot back with "My hair is naturally blond. That hair couldn't possibly be mine!"

Apparently, he smirked at her since she was the only waitress with blond hair in the restaurant. Flo, in a brief moment of attempted diplomacy, pointed out, "If I lose my job, then I'll file for unemployment and go to work at the restaurant across the street."

Since she was well-liked by the customers and the manager didn't want to incur any additional problems with Flo, like her going after him for alimony money, he decided to keep her on payroll.

Flo's been married six times, including the restaurant manager, and her version of why she didn't stay with one man for any length of time was because not one of them loved and appreciated the Gators as much as she did.

"If my husband doesn't know the difference between a slant, a post, or a sweep, then we have nothing in common." She's been known to sniff to the other Lady Gatorettes. "Also, if he doesn't know who the quarterback is or who the coaches are, then we're headed to divorce court." She's been firm on that. Of course, unfortunately, she only dates men during the off-season which explains why she never notices why they don't know anything about the Gators or football.

Mary Jane is a very attractive brunette with a very cute figure and has puppy dog eyes. After graduating from high school, she went to Atlanta for a weekend with some out-of-town cousins. She's never been "quite right" since then, according to the other Lady Gatorettes.

Speculation is that she indulged in some cheap street pharmaceuticals which has caused flashbacks and twitching at odd times.

No one knows for sure, and she certainly has never explained anything. Those out-of-town cousins have never come to visit her again although she's alluded that they may all be in a long-term stay-cation facility for leading others down the primrose path of sin.

Apparently wanting to enjoy the joys and pleasures of a large city, she moved to New York City for a brief moment in time. She thought she was in love with the city that never sleeps at night, and allegedly she didn't sleep much either, changed her mind after a year, and came back to Po'thole.

Natives pointed out that "Mary Jane finally came to her good senses and moved back home." I'm not sure if that's the real reason but, hey, I'm not going to question that...especially since I keep coming back here also.

She also dates guys she meets on dating websites on the Internet. While the rest of the Lady Gatorettes occasionally scold her for surfing for men on the Internet, they are all secretly envious of her.

She also keeps track of Joe D. Savannah's latest profile on dating sites. His latest descriptive creation always creates a great deal of merriment amongst the girls when she finds a new one. She refuses to admit to being a stalker. Her version is that she wants to make sure she doesn't show up on his "you might be a match" notification list. Trust me, she won't.

She also considers it her duty to keep me informed of Joe D.'s escapades. It's annoying...as is Joe D. and his fifty million wives.

Myrtle Sue, a little dark-haired fireplug of a woman, is a domestic goddess. She knows every recipe that has ever been used on the Food Network television channel. She also surfs the Internet constantly looking for new information and statistics on the Gators.

Her husband, while not understanding a single thing about the Gator football team and could care less, worships the ground his wife walks on. As long as he gets at least one hot meal a day he's a happy camper. He also has been known to brag that Myrtle Sue makes the best handheld sandwiches in the world. I guess he would know since he is a farmer and drives his tractor out in the potato and cabbage fields.

Myrtle Sue has a temper. Not quite to the same extent as Misty Dawn, but it's still dangerous. She might look calm but there's a little volcano hiding inside that can erupt at any moment. J.W., her husband, discovered that the hard way.

During hunting season, Southern boys don't believe it's necessary to ask their wives for permission to go hunting or explain why they go off in the woods with other men getting sweaty, nasty, stinky, dirty, and still don't have a dead animal to show for what they were doing over the weekend.

Myrtle Sue had come home from a particularly bad time at Wal-Mart and discovered that her husband had gone off for the weekend with the boys while leaving her a note saying he would see her Monday morning before he went to work. Apparently, it was that time of the month and her hormones were a wee bit on the explosive side. J.W. made the fatal error of telling her that he wanted clean clothes for Monday.

Myrtle Sue saw red. She vowed that J.W. wouldn't have clean clothes for the remainder of hunting season because he'd made the fatal error of not saying "I love you" on his note.

After becoming a graduate of the 90-day Myrtle Sue School of Doing Your Own Laundry, J.W. now leaves notes with a great big "I Love You" on them. Myrtle Sue now offers free advice for marital bliss.

Rhonda Jean is the largest of the girls. As she so elegantly puts it, she's not p-h-a-t, she just has a few extra pounds that have decided to stay with her...permanently. She thinks all of the exercise gurus should be banned forever and women should embrace themselves as they are.

She is the football trick play master. She knows every trick play that has been in a Gator game for the past thirty-five years. She also annoys the heck out of the

coaches at Florida because she creates and sends in new trick plays every week
during spring practice and the regular season.

She very firmly believes at least one trick play should be incorporated into every
game. Apparently, the coaches don't agree.

When a new coach is hired, Rhonda Jean sends him every play that she has ever
created in a Gator orange and blue notebook. She doesn't care if he is an offensive
or defensive coach, he's still going to be the recipient of her trick plays. Her fervent
wish is that one of her plays will be used during a televised game and the Gators
will run it in for a touchdown. So far it hasn't happened.

Her husband, Big T, short for Thomas the Third, is pleased as a pig in mud
and mighty proud of his wife every time she receives a letter from the coaches.
The fact that they are form letters doesn't bother him a bit. He just knows that
one day one of his wife's plays will be used and then they will both be national
celebrities.

Big T gave up chewing tobacco for dipping because "dipping doesn't turn your
teeth as brown" and he's very proud of his big smile.

Your enquiring mind might want to know why I was in a dark studio, my brain
fried, and turning into a lunatic. The short answer is the Lady Gatorettes were
becoming the latest reality television sensation across the country and they were
out of control.

My role in all of this? I was now their manager because I had done live television on many occasions while promoting one of my best-selling crime books.
Therefore, in their eyes, I was an expert on all things tv. Nope, nowhere close to
it, much less on what it took to do and produce a reality tv show.

Misty Dawn looked like she was ready to kill the director. She had suddenly
become very calm, her face was expressionless, but her eyes had turned into
man-eating shark eyes. They were dead-looking. Now I knew why John Boy was
frightened of her.

"Ladies, ladies, ladies," I shouted. "Huddle up." I hoped the football term
would have the desired effect on the girls. Fortunately, it did.

After glaring at the camera and production crew with the evil eye, they sauntered over to where I was standing. Oh, did I mention they were high-fiving each other?

I let my eyeballs drift upwards and shook my head while my lips stretched tight across my face. Yes, they could call me a manager, but it suddenly occurred to me that I was actually the coach. Misty Dawn was the captain. Oooo, the power that I suddenly realized I had. This could be fun for all future adventures. Yeah, I didn't believe it would last long either, but I was going to take advantage of it as long as it lasted.

"Alright, ladies, enough of the trash talk and creating havoc." I looked each one of them in the eyes before speaking again. Do I dare say each one had a spark of hope in her eyes?

"Ladies, these people are amateurs at playing the psychology game with you. We know that. They do not understand that you are just messing with them."

Flo, bouncing her new blond bob haircut, interrupted me, "It makes for good tv."

"They weren't filming then and y'all know it," I shot back. I had to keep these girls under control somehow before they went off in various directions.

"I really liked doing radio much better," Rhonda Jean whispered quietly. She was smoothing down her Go Gators blue tee shirt with the orange print.

Looking like the exorcist had taken over the rest of the girls' bodies, their heads swiveled in unison to glare at Rhonda Jean. I'll give her credit she didn't wilt under their withering stares. Me? I almost wet my pants.

"It was more fun doing the radio show than doing this tv show." She was firm in her declaration.

The director came over to me, let's just say he was never going to be voted for Mr. Congeniality because he sneered at me, "This little pow wow you're having is costing me a ton of money. You need to..."

"Really? Like you couldn't get your crew to work with my team here and that wasn't costing you money?" I snarled back at him. Seriously? Did he honestly think he could intimidate me? I was a Lady Gatorette now and I couldn't be intimidated by the likes of someone like him.

"If you want everything to run relatively smoothly, then you'll let me have a few minutes. Go away, you're annoying me." With that, I shooed him off with my hands and turned my back on him. I was sure the girls wouldn't let him physically hurt me without giving me some type of warning.

Flo slightly nodded her head indicating that he had left.

"Okay, let's stick to the game plan and that is to create entertaining television for the viewers, not creating havoc with the production crew. Remember, the tv audience cannot see what's going on behind the scenes." I prayed that someone was not filming everything that was going on now. That could be ugly viewing. "I want y'all to go back out there, do what you need to do, remember the focus is on the audience not the crew members, and have a good time. Go Gators!"

"Go Gators!" chorused the girls. They scooted back over to the set with their normal exuberance and enthusiasm. It's really called too much sugar and caffeine.

Hours later, the shooting for the day was over. I was exhausted. Even though I wasn't involved in the filming of the show, periodically one of the girls would come over and need some encouragement, a little direction, and a whole lot of listening to why something could be done better because they had all looked up on the internet how things were supposed to be done. I was hoping I didn't look like Jack Nicholson's character in the movie One Flew Over the Cuckoo's Nest because I sure felt like it. 'Rode hard and hung up wet' was a very apt cliché for me at the end of the day.

Before heading back to the tiny trailer I shared with the girls, I decided the director needed to have a clear understanding of how to deal with them. Bribery with coffee and doughnuts worked well.

Leaving the air-conditioned goodness of the studio, I stepped out into the hotter-than-Hades Florida heat and humidity. A hot sauna would be cooler than the misery I was facing as I tried to get my feet to head over to the director's mini-trailer. Stumbling in the scorching hot sand, I discovered my sandaled feet had a mind of their own and had turned me around aiming right back for the cold air of the studio.

Making a swift executive decision, I decided I didn't need to walk an extra fifty yards to his trailer and went back to the studio.

Turned out the heat and humidity wasn't the worst thing that happened.

CHAPTER 2

"**H**e's dead!"

The girls and I were in the small, cramped trailer the tv people had so graciously provided. We were debating where to eat. So far, it was pizza. I was the lone holdout because we had eaten pizza the last three days in a row and I was tired of it. So, we were having an enthusiastic discussion on where to eat.

We had all turned to look at the door when it was yanked opened so quickly. I think the door opening caused a vacuum in the trailer because my ears popped. I saw the other girls kind of shake their heads also.

"Who's dead?" I asked, annoyed because he was interrupting what and where we were planning on eating. I was hangry.

"Danny."

We looked at each other before I asked curiously, "Who's Danny?"

The assistant director, already hyper, looked like he was going to start foaming at the mouth. I vaguely wondered if we were going to need to get rabies shots.

"The director, you idiots!" He almost screamed. "You didn't even know his name? What a bunch of imbeciles!"

Mary Jane stepped forward, with dead shark eyes while looking down her nose at him at the same time, snarked, "Listen here, you moron, what makes you think it's important for us to know the hired hands names?

"For example," her voice was low and icy, "I have no clue what your name is nor do I care. Why do we care if Danny is dead?"

He just stood there with his mouth open gaping. I guess words failed him. He'd look good if he were a fish just pulled out of the water but, otherwise, eh, not so much.

Finally, he pulled himself together and mumbled something to the effect of witches while slamming the door shut. I was pretty sure witches isn't exactly what he said but since we were all hungry, I didn't really care.

There must have been a full moon the night before because all of our tempers had flared up during the course of the day. None of us were going to be voted as Miss Congeniality. I couldn't blame it on the doughnuts and coffee either.

We were still discussing where to go for dinner when there was a knock on the door. Myrtle Sue got up and opened the door.

There was a nice-looking guy standing there smiling. Dark brown hair, blue eyes, pressed pants and ironed shirt, he was certainly a step up from the run-of-the-mill Po'thole man. He introduced himself. "Ma'am, I'm Julian Jones. I'm with the sheriff's department and I'm going to need all of you ladies to step out of the trailer so we can get your statements."

"For why?" purred Flo, almost knocking everyone else over to get to the door. She batted her eyes at him and smiled seductively. "What can we help you with, officer?"

She was almost cooing at him. Oh, just gag me with a spoon! I couldn't believe the change that had suddenly come over her. The other girls were pretty much ignoring her.

He smiled. "We need to take everyone's statement because Danny Durham is dead. We need to know where and what everyone was doing for the past several hours."

Misty Dawn poked her head up over the others. "I think we need to call our attorney before we answer any questions."

I didn't know the Lady Gatorettes had an attorney, although it made perfect sense since the little debacle with Dewitt Munster, yes that's his real name, the local sheriff a while back.

Rhonda Jean grinned, poking Mrytle Sue and winking at Mary Jane. "Let me guess, this is a practical joke by Dewitt, isn't it?"

Julian was no longer smiling, his dark brown eyebrows drawing together. "No, this isn't a joke. You can always call your lawyer but why would you need to unless you have something to hide." He raised his eyebrows. I could tell this wasn't going the way he had anticipated. Welcome to Lady Gatorette World.

"I'm calling my attorney before we go any further." I punched in the number for Missy, my wonderful assistant who handles everything for me and is an invaluable asset to my company.

"Parker, nice to hear from you..."

I interrupted her. "Have Robert call me asap."

"Are you in jail? Arrested?" Missy was efficient.

"No, not sure yet."

"On it." She hung up the phone.

The rest of the girls had gone into their standard Lady Gatorette mode of trying to confuse the enemy which did seem to be throwing the cute Julian off a little. I was guessing he could probably handle them one at a time but all together, I'd bet no one could.

My phone buzzed within two minutes. Turning my back to the girls and the door, I eased to the back of the trailer, all the extra two feet. Did I mention it was a tiny movie trailer?

I quickly explained everything that was going on and Robert's advice was to not say anything. If Julian was going to arrest us, Robert would have us out in no time.

"You're in Jacksonville shooting the tv show, right?"

"No, Po'thole."

"How fast do you want me there?" Read between the lines here, folks. He was basically asking me should he fly commercial or have my jet bring him down. I didn't want to risk us spending the night in some nasty jail so the decision was easy.

"Be at the hangar in thirty minutes."

I called Missy back and told her to have the jet ready to go in thirty minutes. It only took about forty minutes to fly from Atlanta to Po'thole and then about fifteen minutes from the airport to where we were shooting. We needed to stall for about an hour and a half. I was pretty sure Julian wouldn't arrest us in that time frame. He'd probably just tell us to stay in the trailer and not leave. That would work for me.

I clapped my hands. Everyone turned around, Julian looked perplexed. "Did we all decide on the thirty, sixty, and ninety split on the food?"

Bless the girls' hearts...and their minds...they understood what I meant. We all moved toward the door to act like we were leaving to go to dinner.

Julian suddenly realized we were leaving. Holding his hands up in the stop position, he commanded, "No, you cannot leave right now. We're in the midst of a murder investigation. We need to get your statements."

"Not happening." My tone was flat. I was firm in my tone and my body language. I motioned for the girls to move forward.

"No!" he ordered. He looked so cute when he was mad. "Stay put!"

"We're not dogs," pouted Flo while still batting her eyes at him. "We're hungry. We'll come back in a couple of hours."

"No. You need to stay in your trailer until I have some more officers take your statements."

Misty Dawn grinned. "Well, we're ordering take-out then. Do you want anything?"

I swear I thought the top of his dark brown, curly head was going to explode. His sparkly blue puppy dog eyes looked like he had seen a kitty cat he wanted to kill.

"No." He managed to grind out. "Stay here until we get back with you for your statements."

Flo watched him as he walked away. "Cute butt."

"NO!" Everyone shouted.

"What? I mean..."

Rhonda Jean's tone was unmistakable. "He is not, repeat not, your next husband. This is not football season. We've had this discussion before. No more marriages until the guy has been through at least one football season."

The girls nodded and then broke out into big grins and did the Gator Chomp.

"Parker, great way for you to let us know help would be arriving in an hour and a half." Misty Dawn was laughing. "Italian?"

I groaned, "Please, no pizza. I can't handle another pizza. We've eaten that three days in a row. No more."

Mary Jane snickered. "Lightweight. Okay, let's order seafood then."

I brought them up to speed on Robert coming and making sure we didn't end up in jail over some misspoken information. We all knew we didn't have anything to do with Danny's murder but, as I pointed out, sometimes things said innocently could backfire.

"Like what?" Myrtle Sue sounded so innocent.

Seriously? Did she not have a clue as to how they behaved on a regular basis? Every time I think they're smart, an incredibly stupid thing comes out of one of their mouths.

I shook my head in disbelief and then before I could stop the words from escaping my thought process and through my mouth, "You're kidding, right? What about the time...?" I listed off about six things before I truly realized I may have stepped over the line.

They all glared at me before Rhonda Jean teased, "Well, she does have a point but," she grinned wickedly. "That's what makes us a great radio show and now we're on tv. Woo hoo! Go Gators!"

I rolled my eyes. You had to give them credit where credit was due. One of them would always find something positive about what they were doing...regardless of what anyone else thought.

In the midst of them doing the Gator Chomp, there was a knock on the door. Thankfully, it was the food.

Flo stuck her head out the door and shouted, "Hey, Mr. Deputy! Mr. Deputy, where are you?"

Julian poked his head from around another trailer. "What?"

Hey, I didn't blame him for being suspicious. My radar was on high alert because I wasn't sure what Flo was going to do.

"Come 'ere." Flo was batting her eyes again. Please. Did men really fall for that?

"Why?"

She nodded her head up and to the right slightly. "Come 'ere. We have something for you."

Advancing cautiously, I could see he was scanning the area to make sure a bunch of tiny, little Lady Gatorettes wouldn't jump out and carry him off to a nearby swamp.

"Yes?" He was standing at the bottom of the steps, hands on hips. I noticed his right hand was very close to the butt of his gun, probably a safe thing to do around the girls although I knew they weren't going to hurt him. He didn't know that though and that's what made it somewhat comical. Yeah, I have a perverse sense of humor.

"I went ahead and ordered you dinner." Flo smiled coquettishly. Oh, mercy, she definitely had her radar set on this guy. "It's the fried catfish dinner."

His interest went up and his body posture relaxed a little although he did not smile. "Are you trying to bribe me?"

"You want the dinner or not?" snapped Misty Dawn. She turned to Flo and pointed her finger. "You, I will deal with in a minute."

Turning back to Julian and thrusting the dinner at him, "Eat it or not, give it to someone or not, I do not care." She slammed the door in his face.

She turned to Flo who was almost cowering at the tiny table. Flo refused to look at Misty Dawn and was picking at her food.

"Do. Not. Ever. Do. That. Again."

Flo nodded. The rest of the girls were grinning. Me? I was eating my fried fish dinner. Yes, I was watching them out of the corner of my eye. Hey, I needed to know what the protocol was for Flo's lack of good sense of not only ordering an extra dinner but continuing to flirt with the deputy after she had been told not to.

Two quick taps on the trailer door and then it opened. Robert had shown up.

"Ladies." He looked each one of us in the eye. Then looking at the table, he politely asked. "Did you order me a dinner?"

Myrtle Sue grinned. "Flo gave your meal away to the deputy."

"Really?" He arched an eyebrow. "Were you trying to bribe him or date him?"

Flo turned scarlet red. Her embarrassment started at her neck and zoomed up to her hairline. She continued to look only at her plate. Everyone else laughed, me included.

Robert was one of those guys who looked like he belonged in a Wall Street boardroom. Tall, nice looking with a shock of white hair carefully groomed, twinkling blue eyes, and a smile that always looked like he was mocking you, which he was most of the time. He's an attorney after all. For him, he was dressed casually: dark blue pants, white shirt unbuttoned at the collar, and a sports jacket.

"So what do you know about Danny's murder?"

"Nothing." We all chimed in.

"What were you doing this afternoon?"

We each took our turn telling him what we had done all day. Finally, he turned to me.

"You know, out of all the girls, you are the one who had the most time to murder him."

What?! I almost fainted. Why did these crazy things always happen to me when I was in Po'thole?

CHAPTER 3

Robert laughed. "I know you didn't because you are basically a wimp when it comes to these types of things."

Although a newly sanctioned member of the Lady Gatorettes, they didn't have my back on this one. They all snickered, nodded their heads, and rolled their eyes at me.

"Every time you come to Pothole..."

The Lady Gatorettes roared. Misty Dawn raised her hands quieting the girls down. "Robert, it's Po Ho to those of us who live here. The proper way to say it is poat, rhymes with goat, and hole. Poathole. Most of you Yankees pronounce it as Pot Hole which is incorrect."

He grinned. "I stand corrected. Also, I'm from Georgia and that hardly classifies me as a Yankee." He winked and turning back to me asked, "Have you actually considered moving here? You are aware I can be here in about an hour and a half, right?"

I nodded. Yes, I'm still playing around with moving here permanently. Atlanta, where my highly successful cyber security company is located, no longer held the allure and appeal it did for me years ago. At least in Po'thole there was always something to keep me entertained, although it was incredibly stressful at times. The Lady Gatorettes were a never-ending fountain of controlled chaos and craziness. I fit in right fine, as they would say.

I ignored him. "I don't think we need to answer the deputy's questions, do you? I mean, what's the point of any of us killing him when he's directing them for great television?"

"Have any of you ever had a major argument with him?"

Yeah, well, there was that. The little crazy explosion of unbridled enthusiasm might lead one to believe there was a major disagreement between us and the director. I prefer the term creative disagreement.

Everyone looked at me. Oh, great, I'm being rolled under the bus...again.

"Um, there might have been a very healthy discussion prior to everyone leaving the set."

Robert smirked. "Y'all screamed and shouted at him, got ticked, stomped off the set, and came back here to the trailer. Am I right?"

Flo twirled her hair and whined, "It sounds so ugly when you put it that way."

There was a knock at the door. Waving us back, Robert opened the door. "Yes?"

Since the food had already been delivered and it wasn't time for Santa Claus, it could only be Julian.

"I need to take everyone's statement now." He was firm in his delivery. Seeing Robert did not throw him off kilter. That's what I was hoping for.

"Officer, let's talk outdoors." With that, Robert and Julian left us to finish up whatever food might be leftover. Let the boys go do their male bonding ritual.

As a coffee addict, I was starting to suffer caffeine withdrawal symptoms. I could feel my eyesight getting worse, I had the shakes, and I was becoming ill-tempered. No, that is not my normal state of well-being. Being sarcastic is but not the ill-tempered part except when I desperately need infusion from the nectar of the gods.

Myrtle Sue, bless her little pea-picking heart, climbed over Rhonda Jean and Mary Jane to get to the coffee pot. Did I mention how SMALL the trailer was for all of us to be in it? Myrtle Sue started the delicious liquid so necessary to my state of calmness. Okay, you can stop laughing now. I think I'm reasonably calm most of the time, when I'm away from the Lady Gatorettes...and people in general. Okay, mostly when I'm by myself is when I'm completely calm.

The fragrant aroma soon filled the trailer when Rhonda Jean suddenly slapped her hand down on the table. "That's it! I've had it! Open the door and let some fresh air in here. There's too many of us sucking up the oxygen in this so-called movie trailer. We could die."

Who knew Rhonda Jean might be somewhat claustrophobic? I didn't disagree with her on getting fresh air, there were too many bodies in this cramped space, and I'm pretty sure all of our deodorant had worn off hours ago.

We all spilled out and sat in our camping chairs where we had left them from our last pow-wow earlier in the day. Good news was it hadn't rained, the seats were warm from the sun, and we could be outside.

In case you hadn't guessed it, none of us did well with authority figures telling us what we could and could not do. Julian would just have to have a hissy fit about us being outside.

"I need a doughnut," sighed Rhonda Jean, squirming in her chair.

"Since when do you ever eat just one doughnut?" snorted Mary Jane.

"Well, for your information, Miss..."

"Enough," snapped Misty Dawn. "Myrtle Sue, you need to go on a doughnut run but you gotta be sneaky and quiet about it. You need to be back here in fifteen minutes or less."

"Can do" and she disappeared. The Lady Gatorettes can do that on a regular basis. They just seem to disappear in thin air while you're looking at them. I've been told it's just an optical illusion. They haven't shown me the trick on doing that yet.

As bad as I can be without coffee, the girls without their sugar would be worse than any heroin addict in a twelve-step program.

You're talking about five hormonal, caffeine-and-sugar infused women who suddenly went from a small regional radio show to being on one hundred fifty stations within a few months with a national audience of millions hanging onto their every word. Then reality tv came calling.

America apparently couldn't get enough of their particular brand of fun and frivolity. As a country, we needed to be saved now.

To think any of the Lady Gatorettes as a role model for impressable little girls was enough to cause shudders throughout the Po'thole community. The rest of the country didn't know this wasn't an act, this is the way the girls were ALL THE TIME!

The girls were a wee bit more wired than normal because of the additional stress, which caused them to eat more doughnuts. The roller coaster blues of sugar ups and downs created a lot more stress for those surrounding them. They may have been, cough cough, a wee bit erratic before but now with the additional sugar they were consuming I was almost sure any one of them could fly to the moon and back without needing NASA's help.

Sure enough, Julian and Robert came back. Julian was well on his way to having high blood pressure because his face was past fire engine red.

"I thought I told you to stay in your trailer!" He was almost shouting. Robert smirked and winked at me.

"You're not the boss of me," smiled Flo almost purring again, "although I might could let you for one night."

Everyone cracked up laughing except Julian.

"You, you women, need to go back inside the trailer until our investigation is over." He was sputtering.

"Nope." "No." "Don't think so." "Why?" "Go pound sand!" Oops, yeah, the girls were way past the 'I'm going to be cooperative' stage, me included. We were all tired, annoyed that we couldn't go home, and thought this whole thing about us being questioned was silly. Of course, we were sorry that Danny had been murdered but none of us had done it.

"Wait." His eyes narrowed and he looked around at us. "Someone's missing."

"Who?" asked Robert.

"I don't know their names." Julian was exasperated.

"Then how do you know someone is missing?" Robert smiled.

"I know what I saw and I counted them."

"Keep in mind, that trailer is awful small and it would be easy to miscount the number of people in there." Robert was good. Turning to me, "Are all of the Lady Gatorettes present and accounted for?"

Okay, should I lie or tell the truth? Robert and I had played this game in court years ago. We won.

"Present like physically here or present like here but maybe in the restroom? All of the girls are accounted for." I smiled.

Julian ran his hand through his hair. Through clenched teeth, he managed to utter, "How many of you are there?"

Misty Dawn took over. I could tell she was going to have fun messing with him. "Do you mean from the beginning or now?"

He ran his hand through his hair again. "Now."

"There's five of us here. I'm Misty Dawn, there's Flo who thinks you're cute and wants a date with you, Rhonda Jean, Mary Jane, they're both married, and Parker. She's also not married. That's five of us."

"That's it?"

"All five of us are here." Remind me never to play poker with Misty Dawn.

Were we playing games with semantics? Yes, absolutely. Were we lying? No, not really. Okay, by omission, yes, but he really didn't know how many members the Lady Gatorettes had. Basically, we were stalling until Myrtle Sue got back with the doughnuts.

"Julian, you don't need their statements other than to state they were nowhere near Danny or his trailer, right? I'll stipulate to that for each of the ladies. I'm going to be here for several days. Here's my card if you need to call me."

With that, Robert turned his back to the completely flustered and frustrated deputy. Holding the door open, "Ladies, after you."

Managing to hold in their exuberance before exploding with laughter, we crammed in once again to the tiny trailer.

"If we ever go camping together, remind me to get something much larger than this trailer," I laughed.

"When we go camping we never stay indoors except to sleep," harumphed Flo.

"Ladies, while I enjoy your antics perhaps you need to back off the sugar just a little bit." That was from Robert.

And, of course, Myrtle Sue showed up with the doughnuts right then. Do you think the sugar consumption was decreased and the doughnuts were left in the box? If you believe that, then you are probably dumber than a box of bricks.

They scarfed up the doughnuts like starving women on a desert island. The good news was Robert had not tried to take a doughnut from the box because he would have had a hand missing.

I will say I'm definitely a Lady Gatorette for sure because Misty Dawn handed me a doughnut before they were all gone. Be still...and grateful...my beating heart.

"What were you saying, Robert?" grinned Myrtle Sue, licking her fingers.

He rolled his eyes. "Apparently, nothing. Okay, you gals need to go home..."

"Do we come back tomorrow or what?"

"Who's the assistant director or the producer? One of them could probably tell you what to do."

We all looked at each other before I explained, "Um, Robert, we don't know their names."

He looked mildly surprised. "You've been working on this show for two weeks and you don't know anyone's names?"

"We know the catering lady's name is Michele," volunteered Mary Jane. "She's really nice."

Muttering, he said, "Do you know what the assistant director looks like?"

We all turned to each other and shook our heads no.

"Robert, the girls have been focusing all of their many creative proclivities on creating a wonderful viewing experience for the audience."

"Parker, you and I are going to have a talk about the way you're spinning things."

"Took lessons from an attorney." I shot back and smiled.

Ignoring me, although I knew he thought that was funny, he said, "Ladies, be back here tomorrow morning at your regular time."

Turning back to me, "Am I staying at your house or a hotel?"

Since buying the large, gorgeous house on the beautiful St. Johns River recently, I had come to realize that it was really just too big for me. I loved the house, the scenery, the space but, dare I even admit this out loud, I was lonesome. This was weird because I am basically a computer nerd and enjoy my quiet time a lot.

Is it possible that the overly exuberant Lady Gatorettes energy has transformed mine into something needing more stimulation? Am I becoming more of an extrovert? Too many questions, and I probably don't really want to know the answers.

"Staying at my house, Robert. It's big, spacious, and roomy. Your room has a great view of the river."

"Okay, Martha Stewart, let us depart."

Arriving at my domicile, Robert couldn't believe I had gone from a luxury condo in Atlanta to actually owning a home.

Receiving the grand tour, he said, "This is nice, Parker. Did you have Caihong do the interior design?"

"Yes, cost me a fortune to fly her down from Atlanta with most of the furniture but I think it's worth it. The energy feels right in the house and I'm relaxed when I'm here."

Robert laughed. "Gee, I can't imagine why you need to feel relaxed after leaving the Lady Gatorettes. I can see where they would be energy vampires to some folks."

I grinned, "I actually have a really good time with them...most of the time. It can be stressful occasionally."

After chatting a few more minutes, we both retired for the evening.

CHAPTER 4

I smelled coffee. After dragging myself out of the bed, my body followed my nose down to the kitchen where I found Robert sitting at the countertop with the local newspaper spread out. He was sipping his coffee. He pointed at the pot full of the nectar of the gods.

Pouring myself a cup and then plopping down in the chair next to his, I asked, "How long have you been up?"

He looked at me for a moment before answering. "I was told you didn't get up before nine and that you are pretty surly before ten. So far, both of those statements don't appear to be accurate."

I cocked an eyebrow at him or rather tried to cock only one eyebrow. Mary Jane was trying to teach me. "Maybe."

"You also seem very calm and relaxed."

"Probably because I just got up from sleeping."

"This Parker is very different from the Parker I knew in Atlanta." Taking a sip of his coffee, "I think this area is good for you. Maybe not ten years ago but now it seems to be agreeing with you."

"Could be," I agreed, surprising myself that I would actually admit that out loud.

Robert studied me some more, then, "You've already moved down here in your head, haven't you?"

I didn't answer continuing to sip on my coffee.

"Is Missy going to run the company or are you going to continue doing it the way you've been and just physically relocating here?" He sipped some more of his coffee.

"Probably," I finally answered.

"Probably what?"

"Probably just continue with the way it's going right now." I looked over the top of my cup. "You know I don't need to work, right?"

He smiled slightly. "Yes. I also know you have friends here where I don't think you ever had any in Atlanta. You're having fun."

I nodded.

"Do the girls know how rich you are?"

I shook my head no. "I don't think they would even care."

"Me either."

We smiled at each other. "Let's go see what's happening on the set today."

Pink's "So What?" started playing on my cell phone. I groaned.

"Hello."

"I heard you were entertaining a man in your new place last night."

I could feel my face turning red and a bit of anger rolling around in my stomach.

"Joe D., you're still married so what I do is none of your business!" I snapped out. "Plus, how did you know I had anyone out to my house last night?"

"Me and Julian are friends and he called me for information about you since he knew I still loved you."

I wanted to slap the squat out of Joe D. He was my first love boyfriend and the proud owner of We Make Money, CPAs. He wanted to be a big fish in a small pond and that was never my desire. We were not destined to be together in my mind.

He always proclaimed that he loved me and said the reason why he had been married so many times, he was on his third or fifth marriage I couldn't remember which, was because none of the girls ever matched up to me.

Yeah, it was touching. In spite of his obnoxious proclamation of his undying love for me, we had remained friends over the years. He could be quite entertaining...at times...and he was smart except around women who thought he was going to be their golden ticket out of whatever humdrum life they had been living. He married them and had finally gotten smart by having them sign a pre-nup before the wedding ceremony.

"Joe D., it is none of your business what I do." I snapped again.

"Parker, we need to get together," he paused, "for lunch. I may have some information that would be pertinent to what's going on with the tv show."

My interest was definitely piqued. I knew he always had his ear to the ground on various gossip running around town. I was also interested in what Joe D. was doing these days. He was always involved in some interesting investments. Yes, on occasions, we were business partners. We both made money.

In fact, on our very first investment together, we each made over one hundred thousand dollars profit. Hence, the reason why he named his CPA firm We Make Money.

"Come on, Parker, you haven't seen my cute face in like forever." I could hear the smile and charm in his voice. "I'll bet you've missed me."

I couldn't help myself, I almost giggled out loud. "Aw right, where and what time?"

"For old time's sake, let's go The Capt'n's Table. I'll meet you there in three hours."

I snorted, "Just say noon, Joe D."

"Be there or be square."

I laughed, hanging up.

Robert had poured another cup of coffee for both of us. "Old boyfriend?" with a sly grin.

Blushing again, I nodded. "Says he might have some information on what's going on with the tv show. Honestly, I've been so busy with it I don't know what the rumors are. Since he's always got his fingers in something, chances are he'll have some really good gossip."

"Don't marry anyone without talking to me first."

"Seriously? Do you think I'd do that? You'd be the first one I'd call to set up a pre-nup."

We both laughed.

Arriving at the set an hour later, the girls were already there. They had saved a doughnut for each of us.

"So what's the latest?" I was noshing on the doughnut.

"The assistant director..."

"What's his name?" queried Robert, sipping coffee out of a Styrofoam cup.

"Here he comes now," muttered Misty Dawn. "No doughnuts for him."

He marched up to me. Not exuding any personal charisma on his part. "What do you think you're doing?"

Trying to arch an eyebrow at him, the little twerp, "Eating a doughnut. What are you doing?"

"What's wrong with your eyebrows? You people were supposed to be on the set at eight a.m. It is now ten. That two-hour delay has cost us a ton of money. What do you have to say to that?"

"Did you tell them what time to be here today?" Robert stepped in.

Whipping around, the assistant director tried to snarl but it came out almost as a whine. "Who are you?"

"Their attorney. Your name is...?" Robert proceeded to still drink his coffee.

Now the little fella was flustered. "It's, um, Ronnie. Why, why do they need an attorney here?"

"Perhaps you remember you accused them of murdering Danny and the deputy sheriff came to question them." Robert was the definition of calm, almost to the point of being totally bored.

"He had just been found dead." Ronnie was defensive.

"No one told them what time to be back here. Ten seems like a reasonable time. What do you need them to do? I'm sure they'll be happy to oblige you."

The girls all nodded their heads up and down, still munching on their doughnuts. I noticed three empty doughnut boxes. This might not be a great day for anyone near them when the sugar kicked in, although it would probably make for great tv.

Ronnie was still looking a little flustered when Myrtle Sue popped up with, "You aren't dressed right."

"What?" He looked down at his green polo shirt and jeans. "What's wrong with the way I'm dressed?"

"There's no orange or blue anywhere." She did a dramatic pause. "It's in our contract that the director has to wear Gator colors..."

"Go Gators!" "Go Gators!"

"When we're taping and you're not wearing our favorite colors."

"But, but, I'm not the director. Danny is..." as his voice faded away. "Yeah, okay."

He looked around and finally said, "Do you have a Gator tee shirt or something?"

One was thrust into his hands almost before the words were out of his mouth.

"Any clues as to why someone would murder Danny?" I asked. I was only moderately curious because I knew none of us had done it.

Ronnie's eyes were darting back and forth as he changed into the requisite shirt. "Well, I know he had been arguing with the network execs about how difficult..."

The girls interrupted him with various choruses of "We're not difficult!" "If someone would just tell us what you want." "Piglets." Okay, that last one was from me. I just wanted to fit in with the rest of the girls' tirade.

Glaring, he continued. "With how difficult it was to tape in Florida because of the heat and humidity and mosquitoes the size of my fist."

We all started to laugh. "Those are blind mosquitoes and they don't bite. They're just annoying. It's really not that humid right now. The heat's a little wonky but it's Florida. It'll rain later today and cool down." Mary Jane was shaking her head about his ignorance but what do you expect? He doesn't live in Florida. He was a transplant brought in from California, New York, or somewhere. I knew we were all thinking the same thing...wimp.

"Like right now it's really hot and I'm sweating." He was right, he was already dropping beads of sweat down his face and onto his shirt.

Flo stared at him for a moment. "It's only about eighty-three, it's not that hot. Maybe you got something medically wrong with you."

He shook his head, hopefully realizing he was on the wrong side of the battle. "Let's get to the set and start rolling. I think I'm going to get you an assistant."

Great whoops of delight emanated from the girls. This was going to be interesting.

CHAPTER 5

I was curious. How did Danny actually die? Who discovered him? Did he have some secret he didn't want exposed? Let's face it, we all have things in our lives we'd rather not have the whole world know, but was his secret big enough for someone to kill him?

Hunting down Ronnie, I found him going over notes with two of the camera crew. We were taping, or filming depending upon who you were talking to, in a newly created radio/TV studio. The local Po'thole studio where the girls had gotten their start decided they were no longer welcome there. Oh, the girls could still broadcast their very popular show, it just had to be offsite.

The official line of nonsense was it created too many problems to have a camera crew in there filming, the space was too small, it disrupted the rest of the radio station's employees – all part-time one of them – and it took up too much time in the studio.

Unofficially, and far from the madding crowd, the radio manager told me the girls had become more and more overly exuberant in their horseplay while doing the show and had destroyed several of their very expensive microphones. While his advertising revenues had gone up exponentially since the girls were doing their advice show his expenses had also gone up because they were continually messing with the radio broadcast equipment and breaking it.

He was more than happy to continue carrying their show, but they had to do it offsite. He hoped I understood. I did and, honestly, I didn't blame him.

Although legal in all fifty states, sugar was a bad drug of choice for them. Add in the caffeine and their natural exuberance on anything that interested them, well, let's just say I could totally understand his decision to gently move them offsite.

He left it up to me to tell them that. Coward. Surprisingly, they were okay with it and immediately started planning bake sales to raise the money to buy their own equipment.

I shuddered at the thought of a bake sale knowing the mayhem that would enthuse the minute a townsperson compared one cookie to another. A free-for-all food fight would start, no cookies or cakes would be sold, the cops would be called, and I'd have to bail them out of jail. Not my idea of a fun adventure.

The manager gave us a two week notice on relocating the show. Out of the clear blue sky, a tv reality show contacted me about the girls doing their own show. They were aware of the time involved in taping and offered to build a studio set so the girls could continue doing their shows. The radio broadcast equipment needed to be supplied.

Deciding this could be a good move, literally, I wanted to see what the girls had to say.

"Huddle up, my house in thirty. No doughnuts." I texted to the girls. I knew they had just finished their radio show and I wanted to catch them before they scattered.

Adhering to my no doughnut message, they brought pizza and Coke. They can't do any meeting without food, I should have remembered that. I'm kind of obtuse on occasion and some things don't always register on my radar.

Sitting on the back deck watching sail boats on the St. Johns River, we ate our lunch while I brought them up to speed.

"Since the tv people are willing to build a studio sound stage for you to do your show, I'm thinking I might could negotiate for them to throw in the equipment. We're really not going to need everything like what's at the real radio station but we do need the equipment to look like it belongs there." I searched their faces, "You know the only thing you really need are the microphones, right?

"I was really looking forward to us doing bake sales," grinned Myrtle Sue smugly. "I make killer cupcakes and cookies. They are works of art."

Giving her the stink eye, Mary Jane responded. "Yep, I know my cookies will outsell everybody elses."

Before this trash talk could escalate, I quickly bashed it. "Hey, hey! Listen up, ladies…"

They swiveled their heads to look at Misty Dawn who was finishing up her last slice of pizza. She was still the leader and I had better sense than to try to take it away from her. I wanted to wake up alive the next morning…and every morning.

She waved her hand at me. "Parker knows more than we do about this type of thing. Let her negotiate with these guys."

Nodding at each of the girls and winking at me, "Y'all know we stand to make a lot of money out of this. Let's ride this gravy train home as long as it lasts."

Pointing her finger at Flo, she ordered, "No more fancy trucks and no more fancy add-ons. Pay that thing off and keep it for a while."

"Everyone else, if you have any outstanding debt anywhere, pay it off with the money we make. This means paying off your houses, your John Deere tractors, anything you or your husbands have financed."

She stood up, no doubt as to who the leader of this gang is. "We can, and we will, live the American Dream. Let's be smart about what we're doing. I know everyone has a savings account. I know most of you have very little debt outstanding. You done good. Let's continue doing good to ourselves."

Shouts of "Go Gators!" "Go Gators!" and everyone doing the Gator Chomp almost caused me to want to run out on the football field and kill the opposing side. It was a very moving and motivational speech.

Taking our requests back to the reality show executives, they happily agreed to supply the radio equipment needed, set it up with the local station, and life was good.

Because of the overwhelming popularity of the radio show going nationwide, trust me when I say no one was more surprised than I was, they were now doing three shows a week.

The reality show people thought this would make entertaining television. Oh, they had absolutely no clue. After they started filming, I was pretty sure they were going to be sorry they had ever thought of doing a show with the Lady Gatorettes.

The country was in love with them. The ratings for the show were off the charts. Each of the girls now had their own fan club, a group website, were on every social media platform you could name. I was happy because the show had their own people handling all of that. My job was to manage the girls. Yeah, like that was ever going to happen.

Strangely, the girls and I bonded at an even deeper level. We all knew the show wouldn't last forever but we were going to 'make hay while the sun was shining.'

The drawback to all of this newfound fame and fortune was reporters and magazine writers were trying to get exclusive articles on the girls and would resort to some less than desirable actions.

One guy learned the hard way when John Boy, Misty Dawn's husband, peppered him with birdshot after he was told to go away.

Now with the death of Danny, I was pretty sure the media was going to go stark raving mad over which one of the girls probably killed him.

I wasn't wrong.

CHAPTER 6

"Crazy Gatorette Kills Popular Director," "Sugar Crazed TV Star Murders Director," "TV Star, Director Love Triangle Gone Bad," were just some of the outrageous headlines that popped up overnight.

The girls thought it was all funny. They enjoyed the part they were now tv stars and were on grocery store tabloids. They had made the big time.

I wanted to do damage control. Robert was firm that the less said, the better.

We did step up security around the set and the girls' husbands set up their makeshift version of protecting Fort Knox at their homes.

If a reporter, or the murderer, got past the first ring of protection and thought that was tough, the second circle was going to make a permanent lasting impression on them. No, not death, although they'd probably prefer that. Let's just say I'm going to leave it to your imagination as to what would be permanent but not lethal.

Making sure everyone was aware of possible fool-hardy ways of approaching the girls' domiciles, No Trespassing signs were posted every six feet.

These were not the normal redneck hand printed signs. Oh, no, Robert had intervened on their behalf at the River County Sheriff's Office to obtain an obscene number of the official No Trespassing signs.

Fortunately, Sheriff Dewitt Munster was not alerted to the fact the signs were for the Lady Gatorettes. If he had known, chances are he would have led the charge of the reporters.

Dewitt, aka Dimwit, who was a Barney Fife look-alike, and the girls had a history together. He was beyond convinced Misty Dawn had murder on her hands and he was going to be the one to prove it.

The FBI had cleared Misty Dawn of all charges but Dimwit, in his heart of hearts, was sure everyone was wrong but him.

He did chase Misty Dawn outside of Po'thole's city limits but never had been able to arrest her. He had never been able to catch her. Misty Dawn thought it was hilarious he would chase her. It was a game of cat and mouse.

In all honesty, he probably could have attempted to arrest her on the set. I harbored the notion he was actually terrified of her and a lot of what he was doing was just flapping his lips in the wind.

Unbeknownst to all of the Lady Gatorettes, Robert would be their knight in shining armor if any of them, me included, were arrested. I had him on retainer and he was fully aware of their overly exuberant ways.

Me? He was happy I wasn't sitting behind a computer all day and I was out in the sunshine.

My normally pasty white skin now had a slight tan to it thanks to hanging around with the Lady Gatorettes. I was no longer Casper the friendly ghost white.

Big T, short for Thomas the third and Rhonda Jean's husband, and Denny had thoughtfully secured my property's perimeter as well as Mary Jane, Myrtle Sue, and Flo's.

Denny is Denny Rowe, my head of security. He is a former black ops military guy and now heads up all things relating to my safety and well-being. He's about six feet tall and probably in the two-hundred-pound range.

Since becoming friends with the Lady Gatorettes and their husbands, he decided to retire – yeah, I don't believe that either – to Po'thole where the bass fishing is great. Denny also disappears on occasion with John Boy and Big T. I don't ask questions.

Big T was a well-known poacher and may have a certain predilection and skill set to also rig up cameras to spot any potential intruders. Not saying he used that in his illegal poaching but...

I had him talk to one of my techs so they could walk him through on how to hook up the camera feed to my office as well as connecting it to his house.

Big T was beyond pleased as a pig in mud because he was now "doing espionage work. I was born to do this." I think he's been hanging around Denny too much.

Where is Denny you ask? No clue. I'm sure he'll show up sometime. Since moving down here, he's not really at my beck and call any more. Maybe he really did retire. And, honestly, I really didn't have that much security work for him to do any more.

The set was a beehive of activity this morning. Between the camera crew, the girls, the various assorted people with the show, and now reporters swarming everywhere it was an overload of chaos.

Poor Ronnie was drowning in other people's problems while totally ignoring what he was hired to do. Although being thrust into the director's position, he wasn't qualified to handle it. He was not organized in the slightest, didn't have the leadership qualities needed to right this sinking ship, and was cowering every time he was approached. Someone had to take charge.

"Listen up, everyone!" I hollered. The noise level continued. I snatched up a chair and shouted again, "Listen up, everyone! If you don't have the ID badge, leave now or you will be escorted off the set."

Reporters being what they are and trying to out scoop others for the 'once-in-a-lifetime' story ignored me. Well, they did until John Boy, Big T, and a couple of their hunkering huge friends picked up several of the more obnoxious reporters under their arms and tossed them over the locked gate about twenty-five yards from the set.

Everything suddenly became very quiet on the set, although a lot of the reporters were still there.

"John Boy and Big T, escort the rest of these people out of here."

Clapping my hands, "To all of the crew people, all of you wait in the white tent over there." I pointed to a white tent that had been erected in the dark, early morning hours. "There's coffee and whatever else the catering lady has out. I'll be over there in a minute."

Turning to the Lady Gatorettes, winking where only they could see me, "You ladies, go to the blue tent over there and STAY until I get there. Coffee and doughnuts await you."

Ronnie was just standing there looking at me and then managed to speak. "I had it under control and things were going to be fine."

"You're delusional," I snorted. Disorganization annoys me greatly and I have zero patience for it. "How did you ever get hired in the first place?"

His face turned beet red. "You can't tell me what to do. I'm the director and I..."

Taking a different tactic, I softened my tone a little. "Ronnie, this isn't really what you want to do, is it?"

He shook his head no and looked down at his feet.

"What is it you really want to do?" I was actually curious, maybe he could be used in another capacity.

"I really just wanted to be a personal assistant. That's what I was hired for but Danny thought assistant director sounded better."

Looking at me almost with pleading eyes, "I don't like doing this. I don't like people being mad at me." Straightening up slightly, he quivered, "I don't how to do any of this."

I nodded, I could feel his pain. "Okay, here's what's going to happen."

CHAPTER 7

The crew tent had the wonderful scent of freshly baked pastries and coffee. Ronnie brought me a cup of coffee. I was starting to like him better.

After taking a couple of sips from the cup, he helped me to stand on a chair. He whistled loudly to gain everyone's attention. I nodded my appreciation to him.

"May I have everyone's attention? Please take a seat and I'll tell you the latest."

Everyone was curious to say the least. I'm sure most of them were concerned about their jobs. Jobs in the film industry were a roller coaster at best. They all worked when they could because you never knew when the next good paying job would come along.

I noticed the girls had slipped in and were standing in the back of the tent. All of them had their first finger on their mouth indicating they were going to be quiet. I could only hope.

"Okay, we all know Danny was murdered in his trailer a couple of days ago. The sheriff's department has probably interviewed most of you. Do any of you have any ideas why he was murdered?"

Dead silence, people were either drinking their coffee or eating a pastry. I really didn't expect anyone to bounce up with their opinion.

"If anyone would like to speak with me privately, I'll be around all day."

Clearing my throat, that's ladylike for sure. "For those of you who don't know me, I'm Parker Bell and I technically manage the Lady Gatorettes."

Looking around to make sure everyone was paying attention to me, I stated, "I'm also the new director for this project."

Several people started clapping and they weren't even the Lady Gatorettes. Shock and awe time.

"I do have experience doing this." I prayed no one would call me out on this. I've found a good portion of life has to do with acting confident and most people will buy into that fairly easily if they think you are confident in what you're doing.

"Your suggestions are appreciated. However, I will not tolerate negativity, bad attitudes, and destructive criticism. This set is going to be a fun place to work and we are going to create entertaining tv. If you find you can't work in a happy, positive atmosphere, then you will need to leave. Pure and simple."

There were a couple of frowny faces in the audience but most looked reasonably accepting of my little pep talk.

"Today is going to be an introduction type of day. I'm going to meet with each of you individually and find out your thoughts on how to make this show even better. Ronnie's going to give you new ID badges after we have talked. You will need to scan them at the gate every time you enter and leave this area.

"We will have security at the gate and at various points around our area to keep out those pesky, unwanted visitors known as reporters."

Surprisingly, I got a big laugh and a few claps. This day was starting to shape up into a good day.

"Any questions? Nope. Okay, I'm going to start with this table and I'll be interviewing you one at a time in the little green tent. Everyone else, stay in this tent until it's your turn."

Ronnie handed me a cup of fresh coffee. Awrighty then, he could be my personal assistant on the set. I liked being waited on.

Robert was waiting for me in the tent. Smirking, he said, "Good pep talk. Do the producers know you're taking over their show?"

I grinned, "What? You mean they haven't contacted you yet?"

He nodded. "Yes, I explained to them that you could keep the girls under control..."

I rolled my eyes.

"Okay, reasonably under control. You'd keep their expenses down, and you would get everything to them on time."

I snorted. "That should impress them."

Ignoring my interruption, he continued, "I also told them that you had consulted on some crime tv shows and were familiar with the way shows were shot."

Grinning, he said, "I also told them that you'd do it for twenty thousand dollars an episode."

"What was Danny making?" Hey, I didn't want to be short-changed on the money aspect. Women have enough problems trying to get equal pay.

"You really want to know?" He paused, "Fifteen. I told them you were worth more because you could control the girls and," he grinned, "Danny had already complained about how difficult they were. That alone makes you worth more to the production.

"Speaking of which, the producer is supposed to show up sometime today."

"You know," I paused for a moment, wrinkling an eyebrow up, yes they still both went up at the same time giving me that perpetual quizzical look. "I have never seen a line producer on the set. I need to ask Ronnie about that."

I promptly forgot about asking him because he started bringing people in for me to interview.

Two hours later, between interviewing the crew, the Lady Gatorettes popped in. They were their normal off-the-charts enthusiastic selves.

"How's it going, Parker?" "What's happening?" "Found out why Danny was murdered?"

"No to everything." I grinned, glad of a break. "What's up with y'all?"

They proceed to tell me their new ideas on how to improve the show. Some of them were pretty good. I included them along with the crew members' suggestions. This show might end up being great. Well, if not great, then maybe run for a couple of seasons and make us all a boatload of money. Who knew what could lead to what?

Misty Dawn stretched and yawned. "Okay, since we're not shooting or doing a show today, we're going home."

"We're going fishing," popped up Myrtle Sue.

"Wish I could go with you but I need to get this done." Although a day of fishing sounded like fun, I was now in charge of this train wreck and working to get it back on track.

They left and I proceeded to finish interviewing everyone by the end of the day. John Boy and Big T and their friends were taking the security issue seriously. Yes, I had hired them to do security. They were a lot cheaper than a regular security company. Plus, they looked a lot more threatening than the normal minimum wage security guard. These were big, hefty boys.

Robert had already gone back to my place to do whatever it is corporate attorneys do and to charge an exorbitant amount of money in the process.

I hadn't seen Ronnie for the last hour and vaguely wondered where he was.

There was an eager intern I had interviewed earlier in the day who was still hanging around. She was tall with dark brown curly hair, early twenties, impetuous, and seemed eager for new adventures. I scanned through my note cards and found her name.

"Skye! Skye Taylor, could you come here a moment, please?" I waved at her to come over to the tent.

She bounced over. "Yes?"

"Are you still on the clock?"

Her curls bobbed no, although I did notice a slight blush creeping up her cheek bones. Okay, she was hanging around for a cute guy meeting or something.

"You know who Ronnie is, right?"

She turned a little bit pinker. Okay, she probably had a crush on Ronnie. My superior detective skills at work.

"Would you go to his tent and ask him to come here, please?"

She nodded and bounced off like a Golden Retriever chasing a frisbee in water.

I went back to work. Totally deep in thought and not really paying attention to external noise when I realized someone was screaming.

Rushing out of the tent I saw Skye running toward me, still screaming, and with her face awash in tears.

Holding out my hands in front of me to keep her from collapsing in my arms, I don't have that sympathy gene most women have, I instructed, "Take a deep breath and tell me what's going on."

Call me psychic but I knew it wasn't good. Yes, my superior detective skills at work again.

"He's, he's, he's dead," Skye managed to stutter out. "I went to his tent. He was sitting in his chair but, but..." more tears.

Not good, not good, not good. Another dead body and my first day as a director. The media was going to have a field day with this.

John Boy came barreling up.

"Where have you been?" I scowled. "There's been another murder."

He looked me straight in the eye. "I saw someone running toward the back fence line and I chased after him. Notice this red stuff on me."

For the first time I saw he had what appeared to be red dye on his clothes and face. Yeah, I can be observant and obtuse at the same time. It's a talent not everyone has.

He continued, "Just as I was gaining on him, he threw a cannister and it exploded all over me. By the time I got the stuff out of my eyes enough to see, I heard screaming and came back to see what happened. The screaming was more important than chasing someone."

I didn't disagree with him and quickly brought him up to speed on what Skye had discovered.

"Don't touch anything!" I ordered. Skye had found a chair and was shaking.

Quickly punching in 911 in my phone, I told dispatch what had happened.

Since I can multi-task, while I was talking with dispatch I went to my trailer, found a blanket, came back, and gave it to Skye. She looked at me blankly. I opened it and wrapped it around her. Hey, I didn't want another dead body on my hands. Severe shock can have a disastrous effect on a body's well-being.

Medical personnel showed up and attended to Skye. Julian came sauntering up a few minutes later.

"Trying to kill off the competition." He grinned wickedly.

"No competition as far as I'm concerned." I retorted. I told him what I knew. And, yes, I totally forgot that Robert was back at my house and I should have called him first.

Remembering, I punched in his number. He was on speed dial.

"Not another word until I get there." He ordered after I told him what had happened.

One of the EMTs came over. "We need to take her to the ER. She told us she's a diabetic and her sugar level has dropped like crazy."

I nodded my approval. Oh, great, just what I need. Someone going into insulin shock was definitely not high on my list of priorities.

Just because my day couldn't get any better, Julian frowning said, "You better call your attorney. I'm getting ready to arrest you for Ronnie's murder."

CHAPTER 8

"**A**re you kidding me?!" I screamed. Pretty darn sure I sounded like a Brazilian monkey in the rain forest fighting for food. "I have no reason to kill him! He brings me coffee without my having to ask him!"

Julian nodded like he understood. "Still, you're one of the few left here..."

Robert came up behind Julian, tapping him on the shoulder, "You do realize I'll have her out before you finish the paperwork, don't you?"

"I hate big city attorneys," Julian swore, glaring at Robert.

"So you're a fan of small town injustices?"

Robert had him on the ropes, metaphorically speaking. I, on the other hand, was giving serious thought to making him disappear...permanently. It would be easier dealing with Julian than it would be with Dewitt though.

"Julian, how come Dewitt isn't out here?" I knew the answer, I wanted to hear him say it.

"I don't think he's a fan of those women you hang around with." I noticed a slight wince when he said it.

Pushing my luck, I ventured, "So he's scared of them then? Talk to Robert. I'm going home."

And on that note, I left.

Sitting on my deck watching the sun in all of its beauty with blood red, soft yellows, and orange rays waving goodbye to the day and letting the dark start entering for the night, I was wrestling with why someone would want to murder both the director and assistant director on this particular tv show. No one was being paid millions of dollars for the show.

Was the show offensive? Crazy, yes but offensive, no. Naughty language, no. Nasty innuendos, no. Trying to kill each other? I guess that depends upon your viewpoint but, no, the girls weren't trying to kill each other...or anyone else for that matter. Were the advertisers upset? That had nothing to do with any of us, that was all handled by the network.

I mused, I puzzled, I fell asleep in the chaise lounge chair.

Waking up only because someone was gently shaking me. It was Robert, he was smiling.

"You're not being arrested and you're not going to jail."

"But do I get to collect my two hundred dollars for passing go?" I probably played Monopoly too much as a kid with my mom.

He handed me a cup of coffee. God bless him. It flitted through my mind that after three wives one of them must have trained him right on the coffee aspect of life.

Stretching and yawning, I got up and followed him back into the kitchen.

"Robert, what do you think is going on? None of this makes any sense." I told him the questions that had tap danced their way through my mind.

"Who owns the property where you're shooting?"

"The radio station. At the other end from where we're shooting is the tower they use for broadcasting. The tv people built the studio and paid to have the equipment installed. The radio station turns on whatever it is they do when it's time for the Lady Gatorettes to air live."

"Do you think someone is mad at the radio station for turning the girls loose on an unsuspecting public?" he chuckled.

Shaking my head no. "It doesn't make any sense to kill the director and assistant director then. Anyone who would go after any one of the girls doesn't have the sense God gave a goose."

We both laughed. As Mr. T from the A Team would say, "I pity the fool."

My cell phone went off. It was Misty Dawn.

"Go Gators!" Hey, I was using the proper way to answer the phone. She ignored me.

"Are you okay? We heard from John Boy that Ronnie had been killed and Julian was going to arrest you."

I told her what I knew, which wasn't a whole lot.

"Misty Dawn, what are we missing here? Nobody's coming after you guys..."
She snorted.

"There haven't been any threats that I know of. The production is basically still on schedule. What gives?" I was perplexed.

"You know you're next, don't you?" She snickered. "Not to worry, Parker, we've got your back. Later." She disconnected.

The 'you're next' comment had been playing on my mind as well. Did I really want another added aggravation? A brain cell or two must have escaped because someone coming after me no longer caused me to shake, rattle, and roll with fear. Guess that's what hanging out with the Lady Gatorettes will do.

Maybe I should suggest they create an online membership course to increase confidence. Mentally, I started slapping myself because that was just a headache that would be the gift that kept on giving. I didn't need that in my life.

Lost in my own thoughts, I didn't hear what Robert said. So, being the intelligent individual I am, I uttered, "Do what?"

"I need to get back to Atlanta in the morning. Would you have the jet ready for me at nine-thirty at the airport?"

"Done."

After he went to his room, I called Missy, brought her up to date on everything including having the jet ready for Robert, and said, "Find out everything you can on the production for this tv show. Whatever is going on has to be something fairly simple."

There was a slight pause. "You do realize that it's really not something simple when people are murdered, right? This is not a personality conflict that can be resolved by counseling. This is not someone being killed in an emotional outburst. These are planned murders.

"Parker, you need to be careful because, based on what you're saying, you're probably next in line."

A girl can hope it's merely a personal conflict gone bad, right?

"Well, see if you can find an odd connection somewhere on what's happening." I hung up.

The next morning I was on the set at nine. The irony of life did not escape me. I hated being up and facing the world before ten but money will do that to a person and the fact I was doing something new which was fun.

The girls had a live show to do at ten and I had absolutely no clue what they were going to be discussing today.

As wild and zany as they were, they did dispense good advice on marriage, finances, relationships, and doughnuts. Once, they devoted an entire program to doughnuts.

Hoping to receive some free doughnuts, they were stunned when dozens upon dozens of the tasty sugar morsels started arriving at the radio station.

There were cake doughnuts, yeast doughnuts, doughnuts made with soda water, jelly doughnuts, stuffed doughnuts, iced doughnuts. Every type of doughnut you can ever imagine was sent to them.

Why these women aren't kissing cousins to Jabba the Hut is beyond me. I had to quit eating more than one doughnut a day because my jeans were starting to become too tight and uncomfortable. Not a pleasant feeling, let me just say.

To say the girls were in doughnut heaven was a massive understatement. I did notice they started sharing their doughnuts after the first couple of days of receiving so many boxes from all over the country. Previously, they weren't willing to share at all.

They did hand sign their names to thank you cards. I thought that was a nice touch. One I honestly wouldn't have thought of.

All five of them bounced into the studio a few minutes of ten causing me a lot of stress worrying they wouldn't show up in time.

Chattering away, they pretty much ignored me and the rest of the crew while settling down in their chairs behind the equipment.

The radio station had thoughtfully installed a red button on the sound board indicating when they were live.

It blinked red. I motioned for the crew to start filming.

"Hey, America! It's the Lady Gatorettes."

They chimed in introducing themselves. "I'm Misty Dawn." "I'm Flo." "I'm Myrtle Sue." "I'm Mary Jane." "I'm Rhonda Jean."

Misty Dawn took control immediately. "Normally we give advice on all sorts of things. Today, it's going to be a little bit different."

I felt serious twinges of nervousness creeping its way up my spinal cord into my neck. I knew we could always edit the filming, but the live radio shows were out of my control. Only the people in the main studio could cut them off. Maybe I should call them, or, maybe, I should let this play out. The radio show was not on a time delay, oh foolish people. Whatever happened could make for some great publicity for the show.

"I'm Rhonda Jean."

What? She normally never took over the show or the lead from anyone much less Misty Dawn. This was going to be interesting.

Some of the camera crew turned to me for direction. What? Like I'm going to stop this train wreck? I don't think so.

I motioned for them to keep filming. They all started grinning. Me too, I gave them a thumbs up.

"For those of you not in the know, we've had two very unfortunate murders on our tv show. We send out our love and support to the director Danny and his family and also to the assistant director Ronnie and his family."

Looking straight into the primary camera, Rhonda Jean pointed her finger. "For the coward who did this, we will hunt you down and..."

"Give you Lady Gatorette justice," shouted Mary Jane, apparently overcome with emotion. It was really, probably, hopefully just the coffee and sugar that kicked in and was now coursing through her veins.

I was grinning until I heard the ca-chunk of shotguns being pumped. Oh, no, no, no! NOT GOOD! Yes, it makes for great tv, but they were basically threatening to kill whoever murdered the two directors. As my mother used to say, 'two wrongs don't make a right.' I knew law enforcement would be calling me after the show.

Mary Jane displaying her shotgun was bad enough but the other girls had already reached under the control board desk, I wondered when they had had the time to hide anything under there, and pulled their shotguns out. Multiple ca-chunks were heard. They looked fierce until they all started to laugh.

"You see," grinned Myrtle Sue, pointing her shotgun down, "we're not going to kill anyone, but we are giving you fair notice not to mess with any of us or do anything to our new director Parker Bell."

Oh, mother of pearl! I have now been totally identified and outed on national radio and television. They could have just painted a red and white circle target on my back and achieved the same goals. I was going to have a serious talk with them once they got off the show.

"For you obnoxious reporters," Flo was being seductive, batting her eyes at the camera, "I know you have learned your lesson on trying to poach onto our land and get to our homes. Didn't work, did it?"

Oh, great. Now they're taunting the press. Not a good thing in my eyes. I liked the press. They caused my book sales to go up.

"Now, as many of you know, I'm single..."Flo grinned as Misty Dawn grabbed the microphone away from her.

"Flo," she chided, "you know this is not a dating show for you to go trolling for a new husband."

"Why not?" Flo was working on perfecting her pout because somewhere she had read that men liked a sexy pout. She was turning her head this way and that, angling for that perfect pose for the cameras.

Realizing Flo was the focal point for the cameras, all of the other girls started doing their poses.

Misty Dawn ignored them. She was holding up a sign with a phone number. "You folks out there in radio and tv land, we need your help. More than one person out there knows why the director and assistant director were murdered. Call us. Help us find this slurb!"

"Um, Misty Dawn, maybe they don't know what slurb means," Mary Jane said between crossing her eyes, turning her head side to side, and then sticking her tongue out at the camera.

I was cringing and the worst part was I couldn't stop this train wreck. Did I know what slurb meant? Yes. Did I think they were actually going to tell the hearing and viewing audience exactly what it meant? If I had to bet, it would be a surefire 'yes' of course.

Misty Dawn nodded her head up and down at Mary Jane. "Okay, slurb means sneaky, low-down, underhanded, rat, ba..."

"Stop!" shouted Myrtle Sue. "You can't say that on air! Misty Dawn, stop!" She jumped up, reached across Flo thus spoiling her posing for the camera, and pulled at Misty Dawn's Gator shirt.

Misty Dawn half-turned and swatted at Myrtle Sue. A look of annoyance was on her face. "I swear, Myrtle Sue, you ever do that again..."

Flo shrieked, "Myrtle Sue, you ruined my makeup! Get off me!"

Myrtle Sue had half-fallen on Flo when she grabbed Misty Dawn's shirt and was struggling to get back up when Flo pushed her. She plopped down on the floor.

Rhonda Jean was backing up in the small studio set when Mary Jane dived at Flo screaming, "You hurt Myrtle Sue, Flo! You can't do that!"

There must have been a box of doughnuts under the console when Myrtle Sue fell because she came up slinging doughnut crumbs at everyone. I guess she crushed the doughnuts between her fingers because she wasn't throwing whole doughnuts.

Bad enough she was throwing pieces of the doughnuts, she also had icing on her fingers and proceeded to wipe her hands on everyone's tee shirts and then their hair.

This made for great television and the listening audience could certainly use their imagination as to what was happening. And, while it was funny, the crew was about to fall over laughing, I simply wanted to disappear.

As often as I had seen the Lady Gatorettes in action, I had never seen them go full out crazy screaming and dive-bombing each other. I did notice they weren't actually hitting each other with fists. It was all open-handed slaps, slaps that could still sting and leave welts and red marks though.

John Boy was standing behind me when the mayhem started.

"Go separate them."

With total disbelief on his face, he was incredulous, "Are you crazy? I'm not separating them, I could get hurt."

"She's your wife!" I snapped. My opinion of John Boy being a manly man and being able to handle anything dropped to him being a total wimp around women. I was going to have to re-evaluate having him as head of security.

John Boy shook his head no and took a step back.

I motioned to one of the set staff, "Do you think you can separate them?"

He grinned, "Since I'll be on tv, does this mean I can get my SAG card?"

Gritting my teeth, "I have no clue. Figure that out after you stop them from fighting."

Poor fellow ended up being picked up by Misty Dawn and being tossed over the console like she was tossing a rotten head of cabbage into the garbage.

If anyone had any doubts about how strong the girls are, that should dissuade them from getting near enough to find out.

One of the camera crew started pointing at his watch indicating the show was almost over. We started the countdown and finally the set bell rang.

"Cut!" I shouted. "That's a wrap!"

The girls immediately stopped, glared at each other for a moment, and then did the Gator Chomp. "Gooo, Gators!"

What? Had they actually planned this whole debacle? Couldn't they have had the decency to let me know about it in advance? What was wrong with them?!

Seething, I asked, "Was this all planned?"

Somewhat remorseful, I hoped, they semi-glanced at each other. Myrtle Sue said, "Just a touch." She hastened to add, "Not all of it though. Most of it not…"

Shaking my head, "Stop. Just stop. Go home, go do it whatever it is you do when you're not here. Go, leave."

I turned my back on them. Never a wise move but I was pretty sure they weren't going to kill me dead in front of this many witnesses.

The Lady Gatorettes didn't say anything to me and left.

The phone number they had so thoughtfully put out on air was one of the private lines at my company. One of the lines only Missy answered. I was sure she wasn't going to be happy about it.

I didn't hear from her by lunchtime. Deciding I needed to be the bigger person I called her.

Her tone was a little frosty. "Yes, Parker."

"Um, I didn't know the phone number was going to be given out live over the air."

"Do you know how many phone calls have come in?"

Ignoring that, I said, "Hopefully, you have someone else answering the calls."

Her tone was still frosty. "I do."

"I would have told you first if I had known." This was as good as my apology was going to get. I wasn't going to squirm anymore.

She started to laugh. "Do you think I didn't know about it?"

"What, what," I sputtered. "You were in on this whole thing?"

"No, of course not. Misty Dawn called me…"

"I didn't know she had your phone number," I interrupted her.

"Of course, you did. You gave it to her a while back, remember? Anyway, she called and said she wanted a phone number she could put out on the air to find the murderer. But that's all I knew what they were planning."

"Why didn't you tell me?" I was a little miffed but not really.

She chuckled. "Because I know how much you like surprises."

Aarrggh!

"I could lie and say I thought you already knew about it, but I knew better." She was laughing.

Once somebody laughs, it's hard for me not to fall into a good mood.

"Okay, then." I laughed also. "How many calls have you received?"

"I put Sally on it and there's been about two hundred calls. Most of them people just wanting attention."

"I hear a but, Missy."

"Yes, you do. There was one caller, burner cell phone before you ask, who said they deserved to die for what they did to the public."

Now this just got interesting. "Any clues as to what he meant by that?"

"None. I did forward the audio on that to your email. It lasted about a minute and a half. See if you recognize the voice."

We discussed more company business when I received an incoming call. I groaned. "I can't believe it."

Missy laughed again. "I'm guessing your favorite person is calling you. Later."

I pushed the accept button on my cell phone.

"Parker, darling, what *is* going on down there in that little town you're living in?" The voice was bright, chipper, and one I really didn't want to hear.

"Good morning, Saffron."

Saffron Woo, allegedly her real name but I have it on good authority it's actually Delilah Brooke. She claims to be a first generation American of Chinese immigrants. Um, no, her parents are both Jewish and live in Greenville, South Carolina.

I made the mistake of questioning her ancestry one time, she burst into tears and told me she was adopted. I will say she doesn't look Chinese or Asian but I didn't pursue it anymore after that.

She is a book agent extraordinaire, fashion diva, can spin any sentence you ever utter or write into magic. She's an embellisher from the get-go.

If I said I almost died, Saffron would say, "Best-selling author escapes death."

I'll give credit where credit is due, she always gets me great advances on my true crime books. Unfortunately, they're almost always based on what's happened in Po'thole. Yes, this little backwoods, no-nothing town has made me a lot of money. And, no, that's not the reason why I'm giving serious thought to living here permanently.

Saffron always spoke at a hundred miles an hour and had that annoying chipper, breathless voice that so many tv anchors favor.

"Parker, darling, we have another best seller on our hands."

I rolled my eyes since I knew she couldn't see me.

"Are you next on the death list?"

"I hope not because you wouldn't be getting any more books from me." I sort of chuckled.

"Darling, that's true and you know I would never wish anything bad on you." She inhaled a small amount of air, continuing, "Have you thought about keeping a journal while you're doing that tv show? That way if anything happens..."

"A best-selling book could be made after my death," I finished her sentence.

"I wouldn't have put it in those words but, in a nutshell, yes."

"Saffron, I really need to run. I'll catch up with you later." I disconnected her. I knew she meant well and she always made me a lot of money but she was an energy vampire and I could feel my life force being sucked out of me the longer I was on the phone with her. I needed my energy for other things, like keeping safe and keeping the tv show on track.

Where was Denny? Much as I hated to admit it, I needed him for security not only on the set but also for my personal safety.

I texted him. "Where u b? Need ur skills."

He had disappeared after helping John Boy set up the security systems around all of our houses. I thought of him as a more intellectual version of Rambo.

"Wassup?"

"Need to c u n person." Yes, I could text like the kids. Hard to read for an adult, incredibly easy for kids.

"Behind you."

Turning around, there he was. We smiled at each other.

"'Bout time you showed up."

"Fishing."

"Yeah, I don't believe that."

"You should because that's what I've been doing. Plus, fixing up my place."

That could mean anything from painting to setting up explosives around his house.

I quickly told him everything that was going on. "I'm also a wee bit concerned about John Boy heading up security. He's got some of his boys guarding the fence line and, yet, somehow, we've had another murder under his watch. He now thinks he's in your league."

Denny had his poker face on, not saying anything, I did see one muscle along his jawline twitch. I couldn't tell if that was a laugh twitch or an annoyance twitch.

"I'll take care of it, him, everything. I do think I need to be relatively near you at all times. These guys had their throats slit, right?"

I nodded.

"It was personal, quick and quiet. Chances are whoever did it was hiding in their trailer..."

"It was in their tent. Tents are larger than the trailers."

"Okay, a tent makes it much easier for someone to slip in and out without being caught." He looked at me. "Parker, this means it's probably someone on the set who did this. You need to be really careful."

"Wait, wait. Hold up a minute. If the caller said they deserved to die because of what they had done to the public, wouldn't all of the Lady Gatorettes be major targets?" I started to laugh, "I mean, look at their craziness. You could make a point that their shenanigans are encouraging others to have a total lack of control and no responsibility for their actions."

"Whatever is going on has nothing to do with them." He was firm in his conviction. "It either has to do with the director and assistant director personally or whatever his perceived idea is of what those positions represent in the industry."

"It could be a woman doing it." I was all about equal opportunity of accusation.

"It's not. If it's what he believes about the position, then you're next in line. That's the reason why I need to be near you," he paused, "not John Boy."

I nodded.

"I need some of my guys here, not the redneck mafia." He grinned, "I can explain everything to John Boy and Big T where they can accept the changes."

Smiling, I said, "Better it comes from you than me. By the way, you do know that those two are giving serious consideration to opening their own security company, right?"

At least he didn't laugh out loud. He did, however, roll his eyes up and slightly shook his head. "I'll take care of it. Get back to your editing or whatever it is you do."

Turning and looking around, he said, "Parker, I want you to stay in a crowd of people at all times unless," he pointed his finger at me, "you're with any of the Lady Gatorettes. They will kill for you."

I swallowed and then tried to make a joke, "What? Their husbands won't protect me."

Taking a deep breath and letting it out slowly, "The girls have more of a vested interest in you than the guys do."

"You do know I can take care of myself, right?"

Grinning, he said, "Seriously, Parker, anything nerd-like, yes; but, in hand-to-hand combat, no." Holding up his hand before I could protest, "Just because you've taken self-protection classes does not mean you'll do well in a real-world situation of life and death."

"You're fired!"

Grinning, he waved at me and left.

Unfortunately, I tended to agree with him. I was good in classes, but did I ever want to practice those skills in a potentially deadly situation? No, never, and cough cough, I might freeze up. That would not be a good thing.

Any of the Lady Gatorettes, on the other hand, were more than willing to jump in there and show off their knowledge. They should have joined the Marines – swift, silent, and deadly.

The rest of the day went smoothly...until detective Julian showed up.

CHAPTER 9

Julian stuck his head inside my tent. He smiled, "Might I have a word with you?"

Me, being the ever-gracious hostess, retorted, "Are you here to arrest me?"

"Nope. I came to share some information with you."

"Really?" I was dubious, law enforcement didn't normally share information. My internal radar was not going crazy so maybe he was going to be helpful.

He sat down in the metal folding chair in next to the table. Crossing one leg over the other and picking an invisible piece of lint off his pants leg, he asked, "Did you know there was a connection between Danny and Ronnie?"

I shook my head no. "What? You mean like boyfriends?"

He laughed. "No. Did you know they had worked together on some independent tv shows that never made it on tv?"

"You mean like the shows got canceled or do you mean they never made it on air?" I was curious. I hadn't bothered to check my email or messages from Missy so it was quite possible she passed along that information or maybe even more.

"Never made it to air. Danny apparently had the reputation as being able to put together ideas and get funding but didn't do well in actually directing the shows."

"Wait, wait!" I held up my hands. "That means he would be an executive producer then not a director. Why did he end up being a director?"

Shrugging, Julian answered, "I don't know what all these titles and their job responsibilities are, but I did find out that anything Danny worked on he had to be the director."

"Because everyone wants to be the director." Even with all of the various tv shows I had been interviewed on, it always seemed like there were at least two people hanging around who wanted to be directors.

I had even been asked on several occasions if I knew of any openings from the last show I had been interviewed. Foolish people! What would an interviewee know about a director's job opening? They apparently thought I had way more influence that what I was giving myself credit for.

I could understand the fascination with being a movie director but a tv director simply didn't have the same social status in the world. Just saying.

"What was the connection on these sets between them then? I don't understand."

"I don't either," Julian admitted. "I did find out Ronnie came on the scene as a gopher at one of the shows and then Danny promoted him to assistant director."

"Wait! Ronnie told me Danny had made him an assistant director and Ronnie just wanted to be a personal assistant because he knew nothing about directing. He didn't like being in charge of people.

"Either Ronnie lied to me, which I don't think he did, or are you sure it's the same Ronnie on those other shows?" Thinking out loud, I mused, "Maybe it's not the same Ronnie, maybe it's a different guy but with the same name."

Scratching his head, "It's a thought. They did know each other before this show though, right?"

"Yes, Ronnie told me he was Danny's personal assistant, Danny brought him to the set and thought it would look more professional if Ronnie had the title assistant director. That's all I know.

"When I took over as director, Ronnie wanted to know if he could be my personal assistant. I must say he was great at making sure I had enough coffee and he did organize the staff to come talk to me after our big tent meeting. Other than that, I knew next to nothing about him. What about his next of kin?"

"Can't find any."

"What about Danny then?"

"No one really knows anything about him. He might have come from the Midwest somewhere, but no one remembers where. He may or may not have been married back in his late teens or early twenties.

"There's just a lot of speculation on both these guys but it's like they're ghosts in the wind. I've run backgrounds on both of them and nothing."

"Perhaps they changed their names," I added hopefully. "A lot of movie and tv people do that."

"Doesn't show up in any of the organizations they belong to." He cleared his throat. "This is a perfect industry to get into if you wanted to change your name, your identity, and become someone totally different. You're hiding in plain sight."

"True," I agreed. "Once you change your name and maybe even where you come from all people do is say so-and-so looks like this guy I used to know in high school and they promptly forget about it.

"I'm thinking we need to see how many of this crew has worked with Danny in the past and if they remember anything odd that happened on the set."

Julian grinned. "It's what I was hoping you'd say. I'd like to sit in on the interviews."

My hackles rose up. He had set me up. I was more irritated at myself for not catching him at it earlier. "First, I'm not conducting interviews. I'll just talk to the crew in the normal course of events and, second, you're not sitting in on anything. Third, you want me to do your job for you and that ain't happening."

"Hey," he protested, "I shared information with you."

"Nothing I couldn't have found out online myself." I retorted. I sure as heck wasn't going to tell him Missy was doing background checks on everyone. "Also, as of right now, you're off-limits on the set."

Denny had been watching and listening to everything that was going on in the tent and had very quietly come in. I motioned for him to come forward.

Julian turned to see who I was waving at. He frowned slightly. Did he know Denny?

"You'll need to leave now." Denny said in a monotone. "The gentleman outside will escort you to your vehicle."

Julian turned a slight shade of red, nodded, and walked out.

Denny grinned, "You're getting slow on picking up clues that this turkey was trying to set you up for info."

"Ugh, don't remind me. I was actually more upset at myself about that than the fact he was doing it. By the way, do you know him? I saw him frown when you came in."

Denny shook his head. "It was probably because you had someone else come in."

I noticed Denny didn't actually answer my question. I'd have Missy look into it. As much as she liked Denny, I knew she'd also never say anything to him about it until long after the fact, if ever.

I went to my daily work on the set and getting things organized. Denny was never more than several feet away from me at any time. I did notice some new faces on the set. Looking at Denny each time, I lifted my eyebrows slightly and Denny would blink his eyes indicating they were part of his security team.

The Lady Gatorettes roamed off and on the property at will. I'm guessing they were doing their own version of detective work. I'd bet them against Julian any day of the week.

Next morning, they all burst onto the studio set chattering and laughing. The doughnuts and coffee were carefully placed near the console ready to be consumed during the live show.

The crew was standing by waiting for the show to begin. I did notice the camera crew were wearing plastic green army helmets. I grinned and gave them a thumbs up. As usual, I had absolutely no clue what the show's topic was and, honestly, it didn't really make any difference to me because good luck to whoever tried to make them change it in any way. It sure wasn't going to be me.

"Five, four, three, two, one, live!" shouted the floor manager and pointed at them.

"Hey, hey, it's the Lady Gatorettes." They introduced themselves and the show was rolling.

"Today we're going to talk about online dating," said Flo smiling with her pouty lips and batting her heavily made up eyes at the camera.

"Yeah, I want to know why you haven't done that," feigning innocence as Myrtle Sue bit into a doughnut. "You've been married so many times you..."

"This isn't about me, you silly." Flo was still preening this way and that working on her best angle for the camera.

Mary Jane held up a piece of paper. "For those of you in radio land who can't see, I have a fan letter for..." The girls drum-rolled their hands on the console. "Flo."

Flo was surprised. She's not that good an actress so I knew she was taken totally off-guard with this announcement.

Mary Jane grinned wickedly and gloated, "Let me read this fan letter. Flo, you may have a new husband here pretty soon."

Flo shot her a dirty look.

"Here goes. Hello, Lady Gatorettes, my name is Gator Tom. I'm a home-raised Florida boy, fifty-five years old who was raised in the backwoods of Florida. Didn't have much schooling, actually dropped out of school in the 7th grade to help my daddy catch and skin gators, deer and other critters to sell to them city folks who like to eat critters but that are too lazy to go hunt. I make my living by outsmarting the game wardens and I do some guiding on the side. I like plain old country folks and help out when I can. You know like when them big city people try to be slick and put one over on a local by taking over their land by sneaky underhanded ways. I'm easy going but it's been said I've shot a man or two for trying to move in on my hunting area. I have also been rumored to cut me a city boy or two for being rude with his mouth. My motto is if you cross me, be ready for a fight. My daddy looked like Burl Ives. Me, I'm five foot eight, one hundred forty-five pounds of half gator, half wildcat. I like my liquor and ain't going to be tied down by no woman but I do have a soft spot for you Gatorettes ladies, especially Flo. I've got the charm of Burt Reynolds and the get-even of Steven

Seagal. I'll smile at you if you cross me and cut you three ways long, deep and continuous at the same time. Ain't interested in no moviemaking cause I ain't going to leave my cabin in the woods to go to no picture show. I would make any of you unmarried ladies a good husband. I don't cheat. I bring home good game for you to cook. I expect you to stay on my property and I'll bring home the bacon."

There was a lot of whooping and hollering. The girls were all laughing so hard rivets of water were running down their faces. The crew was almost in hysterics from laughing.

"Flo," Mary Jane managed to stutter out from laughing, "this is the perfect man for you."

The rest of the girls started to do the Gator Chomp.

"Stop it, stop it, stop it!" Flo had been laughing along with the rest of them until Mary Jane's last comment. "It's not funny! Y'all are just mean!" She burst into tears, slammed down her earphones and stomped off the set.

Okay, maybe the practical joke had been carried a little bit too far BUT it did make for great ratings. The rest of the girls ignored her outburst and continued with great hilarity for the rest of the show. They pointed fingers at each other suggesting who would be the perfect wife for Gator Tom.

Misty Dawn closed the show with, "For those of you who might think this is all a setup, it's not. You cannot make stuff like this up. This fan letter is just one of many we receive on a daily basis. This one just happened to be the funniest. Gooo Gators!"

The girls were quite exuberant after the show. The crew were still laughing and giving them high fives.

"Was that truly a real fan letter?" I asked grinning.

"Oh, yeah, for sure," laughed Rhonda Jean. "We thought it'd be funny to do it to Flo. She's got such a crush on that Julian guy we thought it'd be funny to rattle her cage a little."

"Where is she?" I asked looking around.

"Oh, she's probably gone home to sulk for a couple of hours," joked Myrtle Sue. "She'll be okay in a couple of hours."

Turning to Misty Dawn, I asked, "Do you have any updates on the hotline?"

"Oh, you mean the 'I be a murderer' line?"

I shook my head yes still laughing. They were funny. "Did someone actually admit to killing Danny and Ronnie?"

More gales of laughter. "Of course, they did. We have had five different guys and one woman admit they did it."

"Really?" My radar was spinning. I knew if anything were truly legitimate, Missy would have called or texted me.

"Yeah, well, none of them live in Florida."

"Two of them are in living a permanent stay-cation resort, and I use that term loosely." Rhonda Jean grinned. "If they had escaped their luxurious surroundings, I'm sure it would have made national news."

I'm guessing if you're guests of a state for an extended period of time, you have nothing better to do than admit to things you couldn't have possibly done.

"A woman admitted to it?"

"Yep, but she's also in a stay-cation place. In California…"

"Home of the fruits and nuts," chorused the girls.

Shaking my head, "What about the other three people?"

"I'm on it," said a voice behind me. I jumped. I had forgotten Denny was shadowing me. "There's nothing to those people. Whoever did it was working on this set."

We talked a few more minutes and then everyone scattered off to wherever they go when they're not around me.

Walking back to the tent, I punched in Missy's number.

"Well, good morning, Parker. I see there was another outstanding and funny show this morning." Missy was chipper. "Before you ask, nothing important has come through on the call dashboard except for that one person…"

"And, of course, it was on a burner phone," I finished.

"Yes. Onto to other news, turns out Danny may actually be a gentleman by the name of Ryan Strickland who may or may not have escaped a facility in Illinois."

"What kind of facility?"

"Parker, here's where it gets interesting. Ryan Strickland had connections with an offshore banking group out of Chicago. He did the whole court thing and ended up in a federal prison camp where..."

Interrupting her, I said, "Let me guess. Someone severely lacking in the functioning brain department decided he wasn't a flight risk, duh, he was doing offshore banking, he escaped and was never heard from again."

"Pretty much the truth. What better way to hide from the authorities than in plain sight?"

I agreed. Being in the tv or film industry, it was fairly common for people to change their names. Since Danny was a director and behind the camera, he would never be seen. Pretty clever, but, then again, if he had been involved in offshore banking, chances were he was pretty darn smart to begin with. Getting into an industry where people changed their names easily, getting into a position that paid well, and being behind the camera that was a win-win for him. Knowing the feds would be monitoring planes and cruise ships for him, he did the smartest thing and simply hid in plain sight.

Him getting murdered probably had absolutely nothing to do with the tv industry but everything to do with his offshore banking activities. I'm taking a wild guess here, but I seriously doubt he gave up that activity.

"How long was he at Camp Easy?" I asked.

"About six months," she paused, "Just long enough for them to decide he wasn't a threat to society."

"Did you..."

"Yes, Parker, I checked out all of the guards and maybe," she coughed slightly, "their checking and savings accounts."

I grinned although she couldn't see it. "Using all of my mental deductions, at least one of them is receiving some money from an unidentified source on a monthly basis."

"Well, you can track it. It just takes a little time. Anyway, one of the guys' wives who is a stay-at-home mom and is homeschooling their two little ones is now receiving two thousand dollars a month from a Caribbean bank where the money is funneled through her newly created website where she is a virtual assistant."

I laughed, "Clever. The feds haven't caught onto this?"

"Um, maybe, they really don't care because their conviction rate numbers are up and they look like heroes in the press?" She paused, "You know, Parker, it really stinks when the bigwigs just get a minor slap on the wrist and the guys in the streets selling weed get a hard time."

"Yeah, I know but that's the way the game is played." I wasn't any happier about the way the so-called justice system worked than she was but there wasn't a whole lot any of us could do about it. "Back to Danny, what do you think happened?"

"We're working on it, Parker. I should have some information later today."

A whole new can of worms to dig through.

CHAPTER 10

Julian stood in front of the Lady Gatorettes, hands on his hips. He thought he looked intimidating. As the girls told me later, they thought he looked silly, but they gave him credit for trying.

"What do you mean Flo has disappeared?" He asked incredulously. Apparently he thought they were trying to set him up with Flo.

"We're trying to play by the rules here," frowned Misty Dawn. "She, um, got upset on the show this morning and left. We haven't heard from her in hours."

"Yeah, she isn't answering her phone either," interrupted Myrtle Sue.

All of the girls were visibly upset.

Julian scratched his head. "Since she was upset with y'all this morning, do you think she's getting back at you?"

Rhonda Jean shook her head. "Flo's not like that. In fact, I texted her we were going to call you. That alone would have made her contact one of us. Something's wrong here."

"Um, can she or does she know how to protect herself?" Julian had flipped open his notepad and was jotting down information.

"Well, yeah, of course," snapped Misty Dawn. "We all do."

Mary Jane interjected, "We think she may have been kidnapped."

Julian chuckled. "What makes you think that?"

"Did you even listen to our show this morning?" Rhonda Jean's tone could have frozen ice cubes in Alaska.

"I was busy with other work." Julian had just stepped into quicksand unknowingly.

"Like you're doing so well at finding out who murdered Danny and Ronnie," snarked Mary Jane.

Julian tried to keep his temper under control but failed. "Contrary to what you yahoos think, there's crime in River County and we have other citizens to attend to."

"I want Dewitt."

Everyone's head swiveled to look at Misty Dawn. She wanted Dewitt?

"He's busy being a sheriff," said Julian in a smug voice.

"Okay, but he's going to have your head and your badge when he finds out I specifically asked for him and you didn't tell him."

He just glared at her.

"Ladies, it's time we took care of this ourselves. Text Parker." She looked around at each of them. "I don't know why I let you talk me into calling Julian. Don't let the door hit you in the rusty dusty on your way out."

He was befuddled but turned and left.

"Okay, so much for that theory," snorted Misty Dawn. "If Flo had been watching us at all, she would have showed up when Mr. Tight Pants showed up."

"Well, he does have great hair and cute eyes."

"Mary Jane, not you, too." Misty Dawn rolled her eyes.

"Well, he is cute."

"We need to get Denny involved. Something's really..."

"He's Parker's personal bodyguard."

"I know that! I mean get the two of them here. Rhonda Jean, tell Parker we need a meeting at her house in an hour."

Receiving the text, I groaned. No rest for the good, the bad, or the ugly. I told Denny about the meeting.

"It's just the Lady Gatorettes, right, and not the John Boy and Big T brigade?"

I shook my head. "Doubtful or Rhonda Jean would have said something. Them calling a meeting also indicates to me it's something serious."

Denny cocked an eyebrow at me.

"Seriously, Denny, since we've been doing the tv show, I don't see them much after the show. They know I'm working and trying to make the show really good."

He arched his eyebrow again at me. I hate that some people can do that. Both of my eyebrows go up at the same time, not one or the other. Trust me when I tell you I've tried to develop that skill but, alas, those little squiggly little hairs above my eyes are not cooperative in the slightest.

"Well, I'm trying to make the show entertaining so we keep making the big bucks," I laughed.

"I'm getting hamburgers and grilling them but only after I see you're in the house."

"Fine by me." I smiled. Denny liked to grill and my culinary skills were pretty much limited to making coffee and calling for take-out or delivery.

The girls showed up in my kitchen and, for once, weren't carrying pizza or doughnut boxes. I looked at them quizzically.

"Denny texted Misty Dawn he was grilling burgers," explained Myrtle Sue. "He also said he had potato salad and chips."

Another healthy meal in Po'thole. I wondered if I could hire the caterer to be my full-time chef. She was probably cheaper than me having Missy find someone in Atlanta to come down and do it.

Forget about having one of the Lady Gatorettes do it. That would turn into a free-for-all with each of them competing against each other. Plus, they were too busy with the radio and tv show to focus on making healthy food for me...and them.

After Denny had cooked the burgers and we were sitting around the patio table eating, I realized Flo wasn't there.

"Where's Flo?" I asked, looking around. "I thought you wanted a meeting with everyone here. Or, is she coming in later?"

Misty Dawn, talking around a mouthful of hamburger, said, "She's disappeared."

"Whoa! What do you mean disappeared?" I was stunned and put down my hamburger. "When did this happen?"

"You know how mad she got this morning?"

I nodded my head yes.

"Well, none of us have seen or heard from her since then."

"Not good, Misty Dawn, not good."

"Parker, we went out to her place and she's not there. In fact, it doesn't even look like she went back to her place after the show."

"Did she go to an old boyfriend or ex-husband's place?" My brain was kicking into high gear trying to figure out where she might be. "Is she doing this to get back at you guys?"

"Nope. We called Julian and had him come out to Mary Jane's house. We texted that to Flo and we all know how much of a crush she has on him. She would have showed up or watched the house. He came, he left, and she never showed up. Something's wrong."

Oh, great! Two murders and now a Lady Gatorette is missing. Out of all the girls, Flo was the only one who probably wouldn't kill anyone at the first opportunity if she had been kidnapped. Well, unless someone did something to her truck. That truck had every gadget known to mankind; plus, a few that she had custom made. If they damaged her truck in any way, that individual should be thinking about who they would want to embalm them.

Each one of the girls had their own peculiar trigger point on what would make them want to kill. Flo's was her truck...or talking serious smack about the other Lady Gatorettes or the Gator football team, and in that order. The girls had really short fuses on some topics.

"Was Flo's truck there?" I paused. "Wait a second! Doesn't Flo have a location finder on her truck?"

They turned and looked at each other before Misty Dawn spoke up. "I totally forgot about that."

Denny punched a few numbers in his phone, grinned, and said, "Found her."

"Where?" we all chorused.

"She's out at some place in the Ocala National Forest. It looks like she's near Salt Springs."

"Oh, mercy!" exclaimed Mary Jane, her eyes wide like Bambi in the headlights. "Isn't that where Gator Tom lives?"

A collective gasp escaped everyone's lips.

"Um, Denny, do you think you could find her and bring her back?"

"Seriously? Does a bear make doody in the woods? Of course, I can," he laughed and then turned serious. "What if she doesn't want to come back? Maybe she's fallen in love with this Gator Tom guy."

"Even for Flo that would be way too quick for her to fall in love," countered Mary Jane, brushing her dark brown hair off her forehead and rolling her eyes. "I don't think she would fall for someone like him, at least from the way his fan letter read."

"You never know with women." Denny grinned. We all stuck our tongues out at him. Maturity as an adult is highly overrated.

Mary Jane agreed to spend the night at my house. Basically to keep the boogey man away. Of course, it helped that Denny was leaving Potus. He was a big German Shepherd who was supposed to be my dog but he loved Denny and the Lady Gatorettes better. He stayed with Denny most of the time. Unless it was one of the Lady Gatorettes entering my house, anyone else would be considered hors' d'oeuvres. Potus took his guard duties seriously.

Denny took off. Everyone else helped clean up the kitchen. Okay, so we ate on paper plates with plastic utensils and only had to throw everything out but, still, we did clean up the kitchen.

Ever the thoughtful soul, Mary Jane set the timer on the coffee pot for the next morning.

I was convinced Denny would bring Flo back to the group, everyone's feelings would be restored, and life would be great.

Foolish me.

CHAPTER 11

The birds were chirping, the sun was being pushy and forcing its way into my bedroom, and some idiot was zooming his boat down the beautiful St. Johns River making an outrageous amount of noise BUT I smelled coffee and that was way more important than anything else.

Stumbling to my feet and padding my way down the stairs to the kitchen I discovered Mary Jane not only was up, but she had made sticky buns along with eggs and bacon.

Thrusting a cup of coffee at me, she smiled. "Hey, good morning."

I nodded my head at her as she put a plate full of food on the countertop. I hopped up on the chair so I could firmly plant my elbows and eat at the same time on the granite top.

"So, have you heard anything about Flo?" I asked between bites of food.

"Nope."

I raised my eyes up to look at her. "That's probably not a good thing. What do you think is going on?"

She shrugged noncommittally. "Who knows? Haven't you heard anything from Denny?"

Which, of course, was the very moment he called. "Yeah, what's up?"

"Well, I found her but there might be a slight challenge in getting her to come back."

"Wait, I need some more coffee." I simply could not take bad news without two cups of coffee in me first thing in the morning.

"She is out with Gator Tom. He must have served in Vietnam because he's got his place wired up in three different perimeter circles.

"Parker, not only is it going to be a challenge to get to him but he's got a boatload of gators in between each perimeter. Flo couldn't leave if she wanted to." He finished.

Mary Jane and I looked at each other. "Um, Denny, do you think he's, um, done anything to her?"

"No. He gave her a separate bedroom. Because it's so far out in the forest there's no reception. I wanted to do a recon before I drove back to the highway to call you. Parker, this is going to take some planning. I need to think this thing through. The question is did she go willingly out to his place or did he kidnap her?"

All of a sudden Mary Jane started clapping her hands gleefully and chanting, "Hercules, Hercules, Hercules!"

"What?" I was trying to focus on Denny's conversation. Mary Jane was distracting me. "What does 'The Nutty Professor' movie have to do with anything?"

"Don't you get it?" she said excitedly. "We can turn this into a mega bonanza of publicity for our show." Clapping her hands again, she was chanting, "Hercules, Hercules, Hercules! Wait until I tell Misty Dawn!"

"Wait!"

Too late. Mary Jane's thumbs were doing the Flamingo tap dance across her cell phone keys. Why I can't be that coordinated is beyond me. I can do one thumb or one finger at a time but definitely not fingers or thumbs on two different hands at the same time. I hated her!

"Mary Jane, this could really mess up our shooting schedule."

"No, no, Parker. Even though Flo won't be there, we can say she's been lured..."

"Lured? What kind of real person uses that word in a sentence? That's an old-fashion word." I grinned. Mary Jane apparently did not see or understand my humor because she gave me the stink eye.

"She's been lured out to Gator Tom's place..."

"Wait, Mary Jane. You guys want to be famous. Based on the letter from that guy, he doesn't want to be. In fact, it appears he's happy pretty much by being himself. It would be totally unfair to have your adoring fans descend upon his house out in the middle of nowhere. It also could be deadly for them based on what Denny said about the guy's security system." I made air quotes around security system so she would get my point. "And that would be REALLY bad publicity for the show AND you guys. Everything might be canceled."

Mary Jane's eyes had gotten wide and she was nodding her head in agreement. "Yeah, yeah, I see your point.

"Okay, we'll leave the part out about where Gator Tom can be located. Oh, look, your phone is going off."

Gleeful was an understatement. Son of a motherless goat! She had been stalling me long enough for Misty Dawn and the girls to get the word out to the press about Flo. My phone took on a life on its own bouncing, vibrating, with Pink's "So What" merrily announcing each incoming call.

"Mary Jane!"

"Toodles. I'll see you on the set." And with that Mary Jane shimmied her way across the kitchen dancing to Pink's "So What" and left.

Fudge nuggets! Time to change my phone greeting. An evil thought crept into my mind. I started to laugh out loud. There's more than one way to win a game.

Arriving on the set about an hour later the Lady Gatorettes were already there. They were not their normal over-the-top selves even though there were plenty of doughnuts and coffee nearby.

One of the crew whispered to me, "They've had to turn off their cell phones because the press is blowing them up asking questions about Flo."

Nodding my thanks and walking toward the girls it was all I could do not to laugh. I was really trying hard to wear my poker face. Unfortunately, I never knew when the mask would try to escape.

"Good morning, ladies. I see you're here a little bit early. I'm guessing you're going to be talking about Flo's disappearance." I was managing to keep my face straight. However, everything inside me was screaming to be let out and laugh at them.

Myrtle Sue was glum. "Somehow the media got hold of our cell phone numbers. I've got fifty messages. Everybody else has at least that many. I don't know how they got our numbers."

Rhonda Jean was almost in tears. "I have my favorite Gator players' jersey numbers as my cell number and I don't want to have to change them."

"Parker, are we supposed to call all these people back or what?" Mary Jane was downcast.

"This was diabolical, evil, and wicked. Parker..." complained Misty Dawn.

I gulped. Had they figured out it was me who gave out their phone numbers on my outgoing message on my cell phone? It just occurred to me after this tv season was over on filming their show I might have an unfortunate accident and totally disappear...like forever.

"Parker, I'm thinking we just totally ignore all of the calls, delete them from our phones, and go on about life."

Whew! Dodged a bullet on that one.

I grinned. "I have an idea. Everyone's going to have to go along with me on this."

Seeing a glitter of hope in their eyes, I described what all of us should do with our outgoing messages. I smiled, "We all good with this?"

Shouts of Go Gators! permeated the air. We all made the changes on our phones.

The show was beyond crazy with each one of the girls giving their take on what happened to Flo. Who knew they could brew a government conspiracy on her?

Before inquiring minds want to know if what they do on the show is scripted, let me just say, as good as tv and film writers are, they are no match for what just rolls so easily out of the girls minds and mouth.

So, no, the shows are not scripted. In fact, I'm pretty sure they don't even discuss what they're going to do on the show. They're pantsers for sure, always flying by their rusty dusties, aka flying by the seat of their pants. That's what makes them so much fun to be around, you just never knew what they were going to do.

After the show, Misty Dawn semi-growled, "Parker, we need to have a private meeting."

I was curious. "Okay, let's go out to the tent. By the way, has anyone seen Denny this morning?"

"Scorpion is your guard for today. Haven't you noticed him?" giggled Mary Jane, grinning.

Scorpion? Yes, I had noticed one of Denny's men, at least I assumed it was one of his men, always being in close proximity to me. He was about five ten although he looked slim, I was more than sure he had killed a few folks when he was in special ops with Denny. Denny only hired guys he had worked with in his 'previous life.' He was very attractive, black hair, almond-shaped eyes indicating an Asian heritage, and had a cute smile.

"How do you know his name is Scorpion?" I was curious.

Mary Jane grinned, "Oh, because I asked him. I also asked why the name Scorpion and he said it was because his sting was deadly."

Okay, then. I needed to calm my hormones down. Also, it was not a wise idea to date an employee of Denny's. Humm, I hadn't heard from Frank in a while, maybe I needed to call him and see how he was doing on his weight loss plan.

Frank is a super nice guy and owner of Sudsy Bath Wash, a highly successful car wash in Po'thole. Turns out he owned a string of them. We had dated a few times even though I can be an incredibly superficial person on occasion, say it isn't so! I blame it on living in Atlanta too long, anyway I really enjoyed Frank's company. Frank was a large man, seriously overweight, and he said he was using me as an inspiration to lose weight. Hey, I have my moments where I am inspiring to others...usually not to do something but there's a positive in there somewhere and Frank found it.

Yanking me out of my thinking brain, I followed the girls into my tent. "So, what's going on?"

Misty Dawn stated in her no-nonsense tone, "We're going to go rescue Flo."

"Whoa! Wait a flipping minute here!" I was incredulous. "Isn't Denny on it?"

"We don't want husbands involved," answered Rhonda Jean. "It's bad enough they think they're security experts now but since Big T may know a thing or two about gators and critters, we, me and Misty, don't want our husbands mixed up in any of this."

"J.W. enjoys being a farmer and out plowing in the potato fields," explained Myrtle Sue. She was obviously very happy her husband had not taken leave of his senses to follow John Boy and Big T into the security business.

We all knew J.W. liked to go hunting but I'm also guessing he enjoyed his marital bliss enough not to want to jeopardize it with his wife. Of course, after that training episode of going to the 90-day "Myrtle Sue School of Doing Your Own Laundry" it probably cured him of a lot of things.

"They think they're going to be in the security business with Denny and if Denny's involved in rescuing Flo, they want to be in on it."

"Does Denny know about this?" I asked. I was going to have to follow up with Denny. He had told me he was going to talk to John Boy and Big T."

"Not yet, he and Big T actually got a contract for security at all of the Cheaters Gentlemen's Clubs."

I had just taken a big gulp of coffee, promptly choked and spit my coffee out.

"What?!" I was trying to wipe off my shirt and hoping the coffee wouldn't stain it.

"Trust me, he's not going to be doing that deal. He doesn't know it yet but he's going to re-sell that contract, make some money on it, and go back into construction." Misty Dawn was firm. I suppose I should have pity on John Boy, but I didn't. He was a get-up-in-your-face type of man with other guys but around the girls and his wife in particular he was a wimp.

I'm taking a wild guess while Misty Dawn and Rhonda Jean were pretty sure their men wouldn't cheat on them intentionally, but they also didn't want the guys to be tempted beyond their mere mortal capabilities.

Rhonda Jean sort of grinned and said, "If Big T knows what's good for him, he won't go trying to prove he's a better, ah, hunter than anyone else including the game warden."

She didn't put her foot down very often on Big T but I'm guessing she might have a Come-To-Jesus meeting with him over this.

We all knew he practiced illegal poaching on a daily basis. He had never been caught, several close calls of course, but he hadn't ever been arrested. Rhonda Jean obviously wanted to keep it that way.

A light bulb moment flashed.

"Rhonda Jean, does Big T know Gator Tom?" I asked, snapping my fingers.

"I don't know. Maybe. Probably."

"So, what if Big T contacted Gator Tom and said he found Flo wandering around in the woods lost. She was covered in mosquito bites, dizzy from the heat and humidity, and he recognized her from the tv show and took her back to his house where he gave her his own homemade concoction to cover all of the bites. He let her spend the night at his house and then got hold of Big T to bring her back to civilization.

"Big T becomes the hero, Flo is saved, and Gator Tom can sell his homemade bug bite stuff on QVC or something like that. All of that feel-good story will drive more viewers to the tv show. Plus, the radio show." I thought my idea was perfect.

"How do you know he's got bug spray?" Misty Dawn was suspicious.

"Because Big T's got some nasty concoction that stinks but it keeps the bugs off him. I'm assuming Gator Tom is the same way." I thought my logic made perfect sense.

Rhonda Jean agreed. "True, Big T does have his own special potion and it does keep the mosquitoes off him. I make him take a shower before he comes to bed. It does stink."

"It's a thought." Misty Dawn was noncommittal.

Not exactly the reaction I was looking for, but I knew better than to push them. They'd either decide it was a good idea or they'd put their own particular twist on it.

"Ladies, I need to get back to work." I grinned, winking at them. "Let me know when Julian shows up. Y'all are staying around for a while, right?"

"I'm hungry."

"Rhonda Jean, there's doughnuts back on the console. Go help yourself." I swear they were like teenagers with their appetites, always hungry.

They trouped off and I went back to the editing room. We were discussing the various camera angles and how to best edit everything when Julian stormed into the room.

"I should arrest every one of you right now," he grimaced through clenched teeth.

Looking up at him, I managed to say without laughing, "Oh, for what reason?"

"My cell phone, my official phone, has been inundated with calls today for, and I quote, an official update on the disappearance of Lady Gatorette Flo."

I smiled sweetly. The editors were trying not to laugh outright at the very beleaguered Julian.

"Who gave them my official cell phone number?" he demanded.

"Remember, Julian, you didn't think this was a big deal and we certainly don't know anything, so we gave everyone who called your number." I continued to smile.

"Listen here!"

Scorpion stepped up and over to the side of Julian. "Sir, I do believe I heard the lady ask you to leave." He turned and indicated Julian should leave through the same door he had just walked through.

Julian completely lost his cool. "Who do you think you are to tell me to leave?" He went to push Scorpion, not a smart or good move on his part. Scorpion moved so quickly Julian didn't have time to react.

His arm was completely twisted around and up behind his back. He was also standing on tiptoes.

"Sir, I'm going to help you out the door now." Scorpion was courteous and very firm in escorting Julian out of the editing room.

Dewitt needed to train his deputies better.

Scorpion came back in a few minutes later. "Ma'am, the deputy has assured me he will not come back with a bad attitude."

"Did he come up with that decision by himself?" I semi-smirked.

Scorpion did not smile. "It might have been explained to him whereupon he agreed to it."

I nodded my head and we got back to work.

Several hours later, when I discovered I was stuck in my chair because I hadn't moved in so long, I was trying to get my body to respond to simple commands like 'get up,' 'move,' and 'get coffee.' I finally managed to convince my fanny cheeks I was not permanently glued to the chair and could, therefore, get up unassisted.

Once I was up, I discovered Denny standing in front of me grinning. "It's heck to be getting old and your age."

"You're mean!" I gave sort of a half-grin as I was trying to shake my uncooperative muscles into the semblance of a live human being. "What's going on?"

"Misty Dawn called me."

Oh, fudge nuggets! This was probably not a good thing.

"She told me your plan." He paused, a half-smile on his face, "I think it's a good idea. Everyone saves face, the Lady Gatorettes get additional publicity for the tv show, Flo is saved, and Gator Tom is a hero while being able to sell his bug potion."

"I hear a but coming."

"Nope." His face turned into a big smile. "Of course, I can't believe you came up with that idea all by yourself, what with you being elderly and all."

If my muscles had been the slightest bit loose, I would have thrown something at him. As it was, there was nothing except paper to throw at him and I wasn't sure my arm muscles would even do that. The worse thing that would happen to him would be a paper cut. Yeah, like that would really show him!

"You forget I own a very successful cyber security company and you don't," I was a wee bit edgy, although I really wasn't angry at him. Slightly annoyed, yes; but, angry, no.

Still smiling, "True, but I do save. Plus, I have saved your fanny on a number of occasions. Whatever. Do you have any updates from the girls?"

I shook my head no. "I've been editing. I haven't heard from Missy either." I brought him up to speed on Julian.

"Yeah, I already received the info from Scorpion on him. By the way, was Mary Jane hitting on Scorpion?"

"I think in her own way she was," I admitted. "Would he consider going out with her?"

"Stop trying to play matchmaker," he retorted. "He's in his twenties and she's in her thirties."

"In her prime," I said wickedly, my eyes twinkling.

"They both are," he agreed, smiling. "And before you ask, yes, I spoke with John Boy and Big T."

"I assuming this is a guy thing and you suggested how they should return to their normal income-producing activities." I smirked.

"Did better than that," he snorted. "I sold their new security company for a hefty profit and they're both happy campers now."

I cocked an eyebrow at him. Okay, both eyebrows went up at the same time, but he understood what I meant. Well, I also dipped my head slightly and looked up at him. If I could only train one eyebrow to go up at a time, I'd be happy. It would give me a whole new set of expressions I could use.

"I'm guessing you also made a profit." It was a statement, not a question.

"Yes, of course. I had to put the deal together."

We both smiled at each other, we both do love a capitalistic society.

Missy called. I knocked my coffee cup into my laptop. "Aarrgghh!"

"Parker, did you ruin another laptop?" Missy was trying to keep from laughing. "I'll overnight another one.

"Changing topics, this is becoming more and more interesting on Danny aka Ryan Strickland. I think the feds may be involved in this."

"The witness protection program?" I was incredulous.

"Maybe, maybe not but it does look like maybe Danny was on their payroll."

"Say what?!" I was flabbergasted. I turned to look at Denny. "I'm putting you on speaker phone. Denny's here."

"Hey, Denny."

"Hey, gorgeous. What's tripping?"

"Denny," she kind of giggled...and, yes, I rolled my eyes at their flirting. I cleared my throat. "Urban slang does not come naturally to you nor does it sound right coming from your lips."

"Okay, that's enough flirting," I exploded. "Let's get back to the topic at hand. What makes you think Danny was on the government's payroll?"

"Mainly because he was receiving fifteen thousand dollars a month from a company doing construction work on a government project. Plus, the check came through a well-known federal bank known for its connections with the government."

Denny interjected, "This is a white-collar guy making money from a blue-collar industry. Let me guess, he was consulting for them."

"Yes, of course."

Sarcastically, I sniped, "Any clues as to what kind of consulting work?"

"Nope. I called the company and asked them what type of consulting work Danny Durham did for the company. I was told it was of a proprietary nature. The guy wanted to know why I was asking about him and I said I had been given his name as a possible consultant for our business..."

I started to interrupt her, "Missy..."

"No, Parker, I didn't say our company but used one of our companies in Ecuador. It would be a real challenge for anyone to connect it back to us here in Atlanta.

"Anyway, the only thing he said was 'interesting' before he basically blew me off."

Denny said, "You know this has just triggered a warning bell on the government's radar if Ryan Strickland is indeed Danny Durham. The fact your guy, Missy, said interesting means either he knows Danny is a fake or he's been told to notify someone if anyone asks about Danny. Either way, this is going to get a lot more interesting."

I mused, "I wonder if Danny was showing someone, maybe the government, how to launder and move money offshore where it can't be traced."

"I'm sure they have their own experts."

"Sure, of course they do, Denny, but what if Danny slash Ryan had found a better way to do it. Then the government would need his expertise.

"Remember, the FBI, CIA, and other alphabet agencies move money around like crazy from our country to others. What if our government was trying to figure out how certain groups are laundering their money?"

"Well, there's that. It still doesn't explain why he was murdered on a reality tv show set. That doesn't make any sense at all."

"Missy, do you have phone records for Danny about three or four days prior to his murder?"

"I do, Parker, but virtually every one of them is from a burner phone. Here's the kicker, most of the calls lasted three minutes or less. Only one call lasted five minutes. There were not two calls made from any one phone. Every single call he received was from a different number."

"Whatever he was doing, he was certainly being more than cautious about it," acknowledged Denny. "Missy, check and see if Danny had a military background." He turned to me, "This almost smacks of a military operation, Parker. If that's the case, you're not in much danger because you're only connected to him by way of the Lady Gatorettes and the tv show.

"Ronnie, on the other hand, may have seen or heard something he shouldn't have...or, someone thought he knew something when he really didn't or that he had not paid attention to. He may have just been collateral damage."

What a way to end someone's life by being collateral damage. That's like saying you stepped on a kid's building block, it hurt, so you threw it away. No emotional attachment to it at all.

"Parker," Denny amended his tone and said gently, "his life mattered, both of their lives mattered...just not to the people who killed them. We'll figure it out."

"Missy, have you received any stranger than normal phone calls on any of the secured, unlisted numbers?"

"No? Okay, keep an eye out for that. Catch ya later." He disconnected the phone. "Parker, see if you can get hold of Misty Dawn or any of the girls. I'd like to see how this fun is going to go."

I could only hope everything was going to go smoothly. Unfortunately, with my luck, I didn't hold out much hope on that.

I hate it when I'm right.

CHAPTER 12

"You know at some point we're going to have to tell her, don't you, Misty Dawn?" Rhonda Jean was whispering. Unbeknownst to her, the cell phone had fanny tagged me and I could hear every word. This ought to be interesting.

I couldn't hear what Misty Dawn said but Rhonda Jean's voice was coming through loud and clear. "Big T and Gator Tom hate each other. Remember, Big T said Gator Tom told him if he could figure out how to get through the gators, then and only then could he have Flo."

More silence, then, "Misty Dawn, I'm not wild about us going through three ponds of a boatload of gators to get to Flo. No, of course not. None of us are going to leave Flo out there with Gator Tom."

Several minutes of quiet, although I could hear Rhonda Jean starting to huff and puff from some type of exertion. I'm guessing it was from hiking through the Ocala National Forest out to Gator Tom's house. That whole area was covered in brush and sable palm, not to mention trees tightly wedged together. I surmised they were not walking down a road either, they were probably hacking their way through the forest. I could hear Rhonda Jean slapping at bugs and mosquitoes. Remind me never to go on a cross-country jaunt with Misty Dawn and the girls.

Then, "Send Mary Jane or Myrtle Sue up in the trees, Misty Dawn! I'm not a monkey!" A groan, "I'm not a fat monkey either! Stop saying I'm complaining,

Misty Dawn! I'm only saying what Myrtle Sue and Mary Jane won't say to your face."

Woo! Rhonda Jean had a lot more gumption than I gave her credit for. Standing up to Misty Dawn took a lot of nerve, I usually wimped out.

"Oh, flip a duck!"

And that's when I realized Rhonda Jean discovered her phone was on. Rut row!

"Misty Dawn, my phone has been on this whole way. What? It looks like it called Parker. What? Okay."

"Parker, are you listening in to everything?" Misty Dawn's tone was grim. I debated about answering her but decided my life was more valuable if I did.

"Yes, and I think you guys are beyond brave about trying to rescue Flo yourselves."

A long silence. "Do not, repeat, do not send Denny out here."

I agreed.

"You're going to be our life-line."

"Are we playing Who Wants To Be A Millionaire?" I quipped.

Misty Dawn apparently did not appreciate my sense of humor. "No, we're playing Let's Save Flo's Life."

"Listen, how are you going to do all of this without that Gator Tom guy seeing you and possibly blowing you guys into the middle of next week? Y'all will be gator bait for sure, Misty Dawn." I grimaced at the thought of my friends being eaten by gators. I definitely wouldn't be doing the Gator Chomp alone ever again. "I'm pretty sure you can't do a Tarzan jungle swing from the trees into his place, grab Flo, and be out of there before he realizes what's going on."

"That's what's wrong with you city girls, no imagination, no knowledge of nature," she snorted. "No, what we're going to do is drag a half-rotted deer around to one side of those pool areas at night. All of the gators in all three of the pools will swim over to that side to investigate the smell.

"If we threw dead chickens into the water to draw the gators over to one side that would cause a feeding frenzy and Gator Tom for sure would know something's going on. This way the gators will just be interested in the half-rotted deer carcass."

Her plan was starting to make sense and I sure wouldn't have thought about the gators getting overly excited and splashing around if only dead chickens had been thrown in.

She continued, "We're going to hang around all day observing things. If he decides to go out, we'll see how he gets away from the gators. If he leaves, then we'll get some mud, slather it all over ourselves, get big clumps of Spanish moss, put it on our heads and shoulders and slowly, very slowly walk or swim across the ponds to get to the hut so we can rescue Flo."

I gasped. "You're going to swim with the gators?"

"Parker, Parker, Parker," she chided, "don't you know that gators pretty much rest and sunbathe all day? They're not interested in floating moss, especially moss that's floating very slowly and not splashing."

Well, no, I didn't know that. Plus, there had never been a reason for me to know that priceless bit of information.

"So, how am I going to be your life-line on this?" I was nervous. I certainly didn't want to be on the Lady Gatorettes Olympic swim team on this adventure.

"We're going to let you know what's happening at different strategic points. While we're in the water, however, for obvious reasons, we won't be communicating with you but I'm going to leave the line out so you can hear everything."

"Um, Misty Dawn..."

"Don't even say it, Parker!" she ordered. "Nothing's going to happen to us. The Lady Gatorettes are *always* successful when we want something, and we want Flo back. Go Gators!"

She disconnected. I just looked at my phone incredulously then realized I was sweating profusely. Oh, no, not those ladylike glistening minuscule beads of water some women called sweat that they very daintily blot off with a designer towel the size of a postage stamp.

When I sweat, I SWEAT! Bad enough I was in Florida where the heat and humidity can make anyone question their sanity when going outside in the summertime, this was pure, unadulterated fear on my part. My head had now turned in a mess of tangled wet hair because apparently the Fountain of Youth started at the top of my head and then cascaded in rivers of sweat water running in rivets down my face, my neck, and drenching my Gator shirt at the collar, the shoulders, then down the front and back of my shirt. The underarm rings of sweat were lovely to look at as well.

Oh, did I mention I was in an air-conditioned room and I probably would freeze to death as wet as my shirt was?

Walking out into the bright Florida sun, I could feel my shirt starting to dry almost immediately. The warmth did feel good.

Strolling over to the picnic table area under the catering tent, I sat down thinking through all of the conversation with Misty Dawn. I shuddered at all of the possibilities of what could go wrong but then reminded myself, she was right. The Lady Gatorettes had an uncanny, almost supernatural, way of making things turn out right. Not in the way most of us would do things but, hey, it worked for them. But, then again, I didn't know anyone else like them...and that was probably a good thing.

My cell phone went off. Quickly glancing at caller ID I frowned and vaguely wondered why I was getting a call from the FBI.

"Hello. Parker Bell."

"Ms. Bell, this is Agent Al Brown with the Federal Bureau of Investigation. It's come to our attention you're involved with Danny Durham's murder."

"No, nope, and stop right there, Al."

"It's Agent...

"We're on a first name basis, Al, until I decide otherwise." I was curious about why the FBI was calling me. "Which office are you out of?"

"Which office? Why?"

Alarm bells and whistles were going off in my head. No FBI agent would not answer that question. They were pretty forthcoming about which office they were assigned to.

"Al, who's the SAC in the Orlando office?" I actually knew the special agent in charge in Orlando because I had worked with him several years ago in Atlanta on a big case that never hit the national media.

"Ms. Bell, I'm not playing games with who do you know in which office." He was certainly trying to sound authoritative but, based on his answers, he was a fake FBI agent.

"Al, that's exactly what you're doing by not answering my very simple and very basic questions. Good day." I disconnected and punched the button for Missy.

"Yes?"

I could hear her tapping away on her keyboard. "Trace that last call. Also, Al Brown with the FBI."

"Hold on."

Two minutes later, she said, "Burner phone. Location is in Jacksonville. I contacted one of my contacts in the Jacksonville and Orlando offices, no such person. That name, according to my sources, does not show up as an FBI employee, agent or otherwise. Is Denny or one of his guys nearby?"

I had kind of forgotten about that. Looking around, I spotted Scorpion who had blended in the background. "Yes, Scorpion."

"Any clues as to who's pretending to be an agent?"

"I'm guessing it's one of Danny's money-laundering guys."

"Be careful, Parker." She disconnected.

This was becoming more and more interesting. How and why did someone think I was involved in Danny's murder? Did someone think I knew something I didn't? Was this just an intimidation tactic or was it just a hunting expedition to find out what I knew?

I might not be very good at nature games in the woods like what the Lady Gatorettes were doing but I was really good at ferreting out lies and deception in corporations, particularly with government agencies. Why? Because my company and I did so much business with them and there's so much subterfuge going on any given time that you had to really pay attention to the unspoken nuances of people as well as the more obvious outright lies.

Waving for Scorpion to come a little closer, I told him what was going on. "Ma'am, I am going to recommend we place surveillance personnel in the trees surrounding the perimeter here as well as at your house."

Smiling, I said, "I have security cameras at my house. I don't think that's necessary."

"Ma'am, respectfully, those cameras will only help you if someone is watching them continuously. Otherwise, all they will do is show what happens...after the fact."

He had a point. I did want a proactive protection team around me. My untimely demise was not something I wanted to contemplate right now.

Nodding, "Do you want to let Denny know or should I?"

"I'll do it, Ma'am."

"Scorpion, you can call me Parker instead of Ma'am." I smiled, hoping he wouldn't be so formal.

"Sorry, Ma'am, no can do. I was told specifically to call you Ma'am."

Perplexed, I asked, "Why?"

He cleared his throat slightly. "I was told, Ma'am, to do that so it would make you feel old."

I turned beet red and exploded. "You mean that son of a motherless goat Denny told you to tell me that!"

Grinning, he nodded yes. "Denny wanted to see how long it would take for you to ask me to stop calling you Ma'am."

Clenching my teeth, I said, "Who won the bet?"

"I did. He thought you would have asked me to stop the first day I did it."

Slightly mollified, I said, "Well, I'm glad you won and not that..."

"That what?" grinned Denny coming into the tent and over to the picnic table.

"There are no nice words for what I want to call you," I fumed.

"Use a Lady Gatorette word then." He was still grinning.

"No, I don't curse."

"Since when? Speaking of the girls, where are they? No one's answering their texts."

Arching my eyebrows, "No clue."

"Come on, Parker. They may be in danger."

"Doubtful." I prayed they were completely safe. "I'd bet them against any regular military any day of the week."

"So would I but they're not here and they're not at home."

"Maybe they're just out roaming the countryside. I don't know, Denny, I'm not their keeper!" I was sounding a little exasperated. Hopefully, that would make him back off a little.

My phone vibrated. Unfortunately, Denny could see that it vibrated because I was holding it. Ignoring it, I started to say something when Denny pointed at my phone. "Is that one of the girls?"

"Probably not. It's probably that whacko that called a while ago and he's been blowing up my phone but I'm not answering. Get Scorpion to bring you up to speed on everything. I need to talk to Missy." I stomped out of the tent and back to the editing room.

When I entered the room for some reason my radar started going off. I backed out of the room and into someone behind me. I almost screamed. Turns out it was Denny following me.

"What's wrong, Parker?"

"Something's wrong in there. Something's off."

"See or hear anything?"

I shook my head no. Next thing I knew Scorpion was escorting me back to the catering tent. Denny came in a few minutes later.

"Parker, you've rattled someone."

I looked at him quizzically and then said sarcastically, "I figured that out myself when I got that last phone call."

"There were three bugs in the room. Also," he said looking over my head and at Scorpion, "there was a remote-controlled device under the chair you were sitting on."

"How do you know which chair I was sitting on?"

"Geez, Parker. Did you not realize your name is on it?" The normally unflappable Denny looked annoyed.

"Um, no." I was somewhat contrite. I was busy and busy people do not pay attention to whether or not their names are on chairs. At least, that's what I told myself. "Had it gone off, what would have happened to me?"

Scorpion and Denny both laughed at the same time. "You would have had a burnt hiney!" "A well-done rump roast!"

As weird as it was, and I probably should have been upset, it was funny. I joined in the laughter. We needed something to break up this weirdness going on.

Still laughing and standing up, I said, "Okay, guys. I need to get some work done and I'm going home now."

"It's only the middle of the afternoon," said Denny, glancing at his watch.

"Yeah? Well, you're not the boss of me and I'm going home. Maybe the girls are swimming in my pool." Snarking at him, "Bet you didn't check there, did you?"

Ignoring that, he said, "I'm getting everything else set up. Scorpion, just go ahead and follow her home. Check the house and then you can leave. I'll have a couple of the guys up in the trees."

"Toodles!" Waving my fingers at them, I left. As soon as I was out of eyesight, I looked at the text message.

"We're fine."

Relief that the girls had decided not to engage in the redneck spa treatment of nasty mud, Spanish moss, and non-treated, putrefied gator wastewater, I headed back to my house.

CHAPTER 13

At midnight, my phone pinged. I had gone to bed early, yeah, I know, what true computer nerd goes to bed so early?

The text read: "LG Flo is back with us" and had a smiley emoji.

"Hooray! Talk to you tomorrow." I texted back and rolled back over when I felt a presence in the room. My heart started racing and I could feel cold sweat starting to form on my forehead.

"Too late, Parker, we're here!" laughed Flo, clapping her hands and the other Lady Gatorettes started to shout, "Go Gators!"

Whew! I was seriously worried there for a minute that someone had managed to slip past the sniper in the tree and broken into my house.

"Before you panic, Parker, we disarmed the security system." Mary Jane informed me. "And, yes, we snuck in past your tree monkey with a gun. He never saw us."

If that was true, Denny and I were going to have a serious chat about how good his guys are.

I got out of bed, flipped the bedroom light on, and discovered the girls had gone for the redneck spa treatment. They were filthy!

Although they were no longer wet, they were sporting an unattractive patina of mud and gosh knows what else on their bodies, their hair, and their faces. Not to mention the pungent aromatic smell of gator doo-doo was permeating my bedroom.

Ever the gracious hostess...not! I demanded, "Ladies, showers right now. There's four showers in this house, y'all go get in them."

Myrtle Sue smirked, "Bet you don't know that we have a set of clothes for each of us in your house."

I rolled my eyes. It was totally possible. After all, I didn't check the dresser drawers in each room. Of course, on the flip side of the coin, it was probably a wise thing for them to have some clothes here. After all, it seemed like they were at my house more than they were at their own homes.

"Okay, great, then. Y'all go take a shower. Wait!" I shouted before they scattered like cockroaches when the light was turned on, hey it's Florida and there are small critters sulking just waiting for nighttime so they can come out. "Whoever is the fifth person for a shower, you can not use my swimming pool as your personal bathtub!"

"We're not that bad," Flo giggled, although I did notice they all looked at each other somewhat suspiciously.

"I'm going first," declared Flo and ran to my bathroom. The rest of the girls took off running throughout the house to find their very own personal shower.

Rhonda Jean grinned, "Guess I'll go get the clean clothes for everybody. Good thing you put in that tankless hot water heater 'cas all of the hot water that's going to used would drain a regular tank in a heartbeat."

I agreed. "Nothing worse than a cold shower."

Rhonda Jean stared at me for a moment before answering. "There is but you probably don't want to know about it."

Rolling my eyes again, "I can smell you guys, Rhonda Jean. Let me just say that smell is never going to go in a perfume bottle."

She left and I wandered downstairs to put on a pot of coffee. I found a dozen doughnuts in the freezer and popped them in the oven to warm up. I decided I should turn the oven on low so I didn't burn them up which, unfortunately, I had done several weeks earlier. Hey, Martha Stewart I'm not!

Myrtle Sue entered the kitchen first. Glancing at the coffee pot to make sure it was full, she opened the oven door and made sure the doughnuts were thawing out.

"How'd you know?" I asked, I was still in my long Gator tee shirt.

"Well, I could smell them for one thing, and the second thing is I figured sooner or later you'd find the frozen doughnuts. Even you could figure out how to put them all in the oven versus trying to microwave them one by one." She was busy pulling eggs and bacon out of the refrigerator.

Yes, I know I said I'm not a cook, I'm not! But I do have the basic breakfast staples in the refrigerator. Of course, it helps that Myrtle Sue will periodically make a grocery run for me and stock things up.

The girls all drifted into the kitchen one by one looking and smelling a thousand percent better than they had forty-five minutes earlier. Honestly, I didn't care how long they spent in the shower as long as all of that nasty stuff on them was gone.

"I'm hungry," said Flo and then each one of the girls chimed in saying the same thing.

"I'm cooking, give me a minute." Myrtle Sue was cooking up a big breakfast of eggs, bacon, hash browns, juice, toast, doughnuts, and coffee.

Round one of the food jamboree was consumed in under five minutes, round two took about ten minutes, and round three, I guess the girls were becoming satiated because it took about fifteen minutes for them to stop eating and asking for more.

"Parker, I'm going to need to make a grocery run."

I nodded, swallowing my last forkful of scrambled egg. "Just use the card in the drawer for what you need."

Leaning back in my chair at the countertop, I said, "Okay, now that we're all full, somebody tell me what happened. And, Flo, I'm really happy you're back."

She beamed. "Me too, Parker."

Putting her coffee cup down, she said, "I'm going first and then y'all can tell your side of the story. Gator Tom really isn't a bad guy."

Giving half of a stink eye to the girls, she continued. "Y'all know I was mad when I left the set. I was thinking if this was the same Gator Tom that Big T knew, I had a rough idea of where he lived. I could go out there and surprise him."

One of the girls snickered, I wasn't sure who it was. Cough, cough it might have been me.

"Anyway, I figured out how to get down that dirt road. Thank goodness for my truck because if I had been in a car, I would've gotten stuck in the sand. I got to the end of the road. I mean the road just stopped, I didn't even see a spot where I could get turned around. So I got out of the truck and started to walk through some big bushes to see if the road picked up on the other side. It didn't but Gator Tom was standing next to a big pine tree with a big grin."

She paused for a gulp of coffee. "He said, 'Darlin', I've been waiting for you.' That didn't scare me because he's a man, after all." She winked. "What did kind of make my hair go prickly and all was he had a gator on a leash."

"Really?" I was dubious. "Gator on a leash?"

"Well, he did have a pole attached to the leash so the gator couldn't get real close to him. He asked me to come back to his place and since I was so mad at y'all I decided to do it."

The girls did have the courtesy to look a little chagrined, not much but a little bit.

"We hiked back to his place..."

"Wait. How far was it?" I wanted to know, sipping on my coffee.

"Probably about a half mile, give or take. We get to his place..."

"Yeah, how did you get to his hut?" asked Rhonda Jean. "We didn't find any way to get to it without going through the ponds."

"He had an airboat."

"Yeah, we saw that. Those things make a lot of noise," said Misty Dawn, looking around the kitchen for more doughnuts. Myrtle Sue took the last remaining one off of her plate and gave it to Misty Dawn who nodded her thanks.

"Yes, they do. That's how we got to his stilt house. The gators sort of moved out of the way, although we did hit a few hard bumps which I'm guessing was a gator.

"Anyway, his house is really nice on the inside, rustic, but nice looking. Bad part was no air conditioning, and it was steamy hot in there. I asked him about that and he said he didn't like air conditioning because he couldn't hear poachers coming to take his gators."

"Big T did say Gator Tom was a might touchy about his gators," confirmed Rhonda Jean. And that statement confirmed the most likely reason why Big T didn't like Gator Tom. I'm guessing the gators were good size and Big T could have made a fortune from either capturing them or selling their hides, hence the dislike on the part of both men.

"He fixed me dinner which, by the way, was really good. He's just a good old boy who doesn't like being around people much."

"Flo, how does he make his living? 'Cas even out in the woods, he's got to have some cash." Mary Jane brought up a good point. "Also, he has an airboat and those things aren't cheap. Even a used one can be a bit pricey."

She nodded her head in agreement. "I know and I asked him about that. He said a couple of years back he had gone into a convenience store in Salt Springs and bought a five-dollar scratch-off ticket. He said he won a million dollars on it."

"That's easy enough to check," I said as I was texting Missy to find out.

"He gave me my own bedroom. What he didn't give me was mosquito netting. It's eat Flo alive mosquito season. When I came out the next morning, I had bug bites everywhere. And because I couldn't sleep with the mosquitoes humming and trying to carry me off into the swamp and how stinking hot it was, I wasn't my normal delightful self."

We all groaned. Let me be fair and say, Flo is typically one of the easier going Lady Gatorettes.

"What did he say to that?" laughed Mary Jane.

"He gave me some bug lotion that his mama taught him how to make that stopped the itching. Also, the mosquitoes didn't try to land on me as much. He fixed me breakfast and then told me since I hunted him down..."

"Say what?" We all chorused.

"Since I had hunted him down that meant I was going to be his woman. He had asked God for a sign for a beautiful woman to come be his wife." She preened for a moment, "That would be me. But," she frowned, "I don't want to be his wife. For one thing, he doesn't get tv out there and he doesn't know who's coaching the Gators."

"He does know who the Gators are, right?" Misty Dawn almost whispered.

She nodded, "Yes. He's aware they are the University of Florida's football team. He told me he had no use for a bunch of kids running up and down a field chasing an inflated piece of pigskin."

Well, that just about did everyone in, including me. We all gasped. I honestly thought I might have to call 911. Misty Dawn put her head in her hands in shock. Mary Jane's mouth gaped open. Myrtle Sue had her hand over heart and was breathing deeply. Rhonda Jean just kept blinking her eyes and nodding her head while she was rocking on her feet. Me? I felt the blood drain from my head, and I almost felt faint.

Let me just say, more sacrilegious words could not have come out of Gator Tom's mouth. We all knew that was the moment Flo wanted to come home for sure.

"Then what did you do?" Rhonda Jean managed to eke out in a soft voice. Her fists were clenching and unclenching, probably a subconscious reaction to hearing Gator Tom's blasphemous words.

"Why, I told him I wanted to come home, of course!" She spouted off, "The man's a fool! How dare he EVER say anything like that to any of us and expect a Lady Gatorette to fall in love with him. He's an idiot!"

We all nodded in agreement. My phone pinged with a text. "U ok n there I c lights on."

I relayed that message to the girls and we all promptly started laughing. Not only had they snuck in under this finely trained sniper of Denny's, but lights had been on in the house for almost two hours and he was just now noticing this?

"You know what I think we should do?" Misty Dawn had a wicked grin on her face.

"Oh, no, no, no!" I was laughing. "You guys cannot go out there and yank him down before he even notices."

"Okay, then, we'll let *you* do it." Everyone was laughing.

"No, no. Watch this." I started texting. "You're fired. Leave now. I can see you from the house and I expect you to be off my property in five minutes."

He responded almost immediately. "No can do."

My text said, "I have you in my sights. Leave now!"

Looking at the incoming message, I read it to the girls. "He says and I quote, 'No u can't c me.' Really?"

"He's an idiot," Misty Dawn snorted. She did have an evil glint in her eye. We had eaten, rested, and were still on an adrenaline high. This idiot had no clue what was going to happen to him.

"Flip off all of the lights. Let's go!" I ordered. I heard soft "Go Gators!" from the girls.

"I'm putting my body cam on," said Mary Jane. "That way there's no disputing his incompetence when you tell Denny."

"Denny's not going to be happy," confirmed Misty Dawn.

Since the girls had been at my house so many times, we found the items we needed very easily in the dark. Then I received another ping.

"Turn that thing to silent," snapped Misty Dawn.

I read it. "He says about time I went back to bed." That did it. "As long as we don't kill him, I don't care what we do."

More "Go Gators!" and we were out the door. I strongly suspected the guy probably wouldn't pay any more attention to the house since the lights were off and I hadn't responded to his last text.

This guy's lack of professionalism was incredible. I couldn't believe Denny had ever hired this guy. Then it dawned on me, maybe this wasn't Denny's guy. Maybe it was from the guy who called me on the phone acting like an FBI agent.

These thoughts were running through my head as I was following behind Misty Dawn. Do I dare say I believe the girls must have practiced this maneuver before? They spread out and approached the tree. This guy was clueless!

Of course it helped we were all wearing night goggles and we had changed into black shirts with the prerequisite black balaclava. Girls and their play toys. I never asked where they came up with this stuff. Although, I have to be honest, I was a wee bit surprised this equipment was in my house. They were probably in the same drawers as their clean set of clothes I knew nothing about.

One of the girls, I'm not sure who, threw a rock into the bushes away from my house. It's okay, I don't like azaleas except for two weeks out of the year. The rest of the time they look like big, old, fuzzy green bushes not adding to the overall beauty of nature.

A single gunshot. This guy was shooting at something he couldn't see or even identify? Priceless. I was becoming more and more convinced this wasn't one of Denny's well-trained men. I wasn't sure who it was, but he was pretty much worthless in the protection area, especially mine.

A thud, he fell out of the tree. It was not a natural, accidental falling out of the tree. I was close enough to Misty Dawn to see that she had thrown something around the guy and yanked him to the ground.

"Secured." I heard on our voice coms. Everyone came over to look at the guy. He was dazed and it took him a moment to realize his hands were zip tied behind his back. He was, however, fully aware that he was laying on his right side with Misty Dawn's knee pressed down on the soft spot between his ribs and his hip.

"No screaming or shouting." She ordered, picking up his head and turning it toward her. "Do you understand?"

He nodded. He did have fear in his eyes.

"Who hired you?"

"Not going to tell you," he sneered.

He definitely wasn't one of Denny's guys. The question was where was Denny's guy?

"Where's the other guy that was supposed to be here?" I asked.

He could hear me but couldn't see me because I was out of his line of sight.

"Sleeping," he sneered again.

"Don't believe I like your attitude," snapped Mary Jane as she walked up to where he could see her. She kicked him in the stomach and he promptly threw up.

"Tell me where the other guy is," snapped Misty Dawn again.

He coughed and said, "Told him we were changing shifts. As he was coming down out of the tree, I stuck him in the hiney with a needle." He sort of looked hopeful that no more physical harm was going to come to him.

"Where. Is. He?" Misty Dawn's tone was deadly. She increased her knee pressure.

"Hey, it's becoming harder for me to breathe."

"Yeah, I know. Where. Is. He?"

"Wouldn't you like to know?" He grinned, daring them to do something. Foolish man.

Misty Dawn stood up, grabbed him by the back of his uniform, and was dragging him back to my house.

He was struggling trying to get to his feet and was failing. "Where are you taking me?"

No answer. I had a very strong suspicion he was going to be introduced to the very large baptismal font at my house; otherwise, known as the swimming pool. I was pretty sure the girls weren't going to waterboard him. It was probably more effective for the guy to actually believe he was going to drown. At least I had my fingers crossed that the girls weren't actually going to drown him. Fear can be a powerful motivator to get someone to talk.

Misty Dawn continued dragging him through the lawn, opened the screen door to the patio and swimming pool area, and threw him in the pool.

He bounced up and started screaming all sorts of naughty words at us.

Misty Dawn glared down at him in the pool. "We can do this the easy way or the hard way. Once you've made your decision, that's it. You're not getting a second chance."

"Um, you might want to tell him the hard way is going to be torture and death," Mary Jane offered up. "By the way, Mr. Whoever you are, I get first choice if you decide the hard way."

I gulped. Maybe they were going to kill this guy.

Turning to me and winking where the hapless piece of human being couldn't see her, Myrtle Sue said, "We'll drain the pool and clean the blood out when we're through."

I nodded my head in agreement. Finally finding my voice, I shrugged, "Yeah, that last guy was a mess getting the pool cleaned up. I thought the blood was never going to come out."

The guy started shouting again. "You can't kill me! You don't know who you're messing with!"

"So tell us," grinned Misty Dawn sitting down in a chair by the pool's edge.

Rhonda Jean had disappeared for a few minutes and returned holding the guy's cell phone and his AR-18 assault rifle.

"Oh, lookey, lookey. What do we have here?" Misty Dawn grinned diabolically. "A cell phone with all sorts of numbers in them. Oh, look. Several calls to one number in the past three hours. I think I need to call that one."

"No, no!" shouted the guy, panicking, bouncing up and down in the water. "I'll be killed!"

Misty Dawn checked the gun's magazine, snapped it back into place, and then fired the gun at the guy. I flinched thinking she had just shot an unarmed man in my swimming pool. I wasn't sure how Robert was going to keep me out of jail on this.

He screamed, "You shot me! You shot me! I'm dying!" and proceeded spew out more language you would never ever hear in a Baptist church, even the more liberal ones.

Flo laughed and said, "You fool! If she had wanted you dead, you'd be dead."

He finally looked down at himself and realized he wasn't bleeding. He started to laugh, "Yeah, I didn't think you had the..."

Mary Jane had found the volleyball we played with in the pool and nailed him in the head with it. He immediately sank under the water.

I started to freak out. "He's going to drown!"

"Nah, he won't. He'll be spitting and cursing when he bobs back to the surface. A couple of more hits like that, he's going to start to talk." Misty Dawn was still totally relaxed sitting in the chair.

Mary Jane extracted the ball out of the water with the skimmer head net pole. It's Florida and every swimming pool has one; plus, a boathook to save swimmers.

As soon as the guy bobbed to the top, Mary Jane slammed him in the middle of the face with the ball. I saw blood in the water. She had broken his nose and with the force she'd thrown the ball, he probably had a concussion too.

Note to self, always, always, always play on Mary Jane's water volleyball team.

He slowly came back up to the surface of the water. He was trying hard to keep his head above water. Instead of moving forward into more shallow water, he had backed into the deeper part of the pool.

"Mumph, salph."

"Can't hear you!" shouted Misty Dawn. Myrtle Sue had thoughtfully brought out chips, salsa, and cokes and placed them on the patio table where we could snack on them. We all were helping ourselves with a little bit of glee.

I could tell the guy was almost ready to talk since he was struggling to stay above water.

Mary Jane winked at me and reared back to throw the volleyball at him again when he finally tried to shout, "Stop. Just stop, I'll tell you."

"You sure?" laughed Misty Dawn. "'Cas if you're lying, you're dying."

"Just shoot me and get it over with," he said dejectedly,

still trying to keep his head above water.

"Fish him out."

Mary Jane took the boat hook and poked him forward until he was at the bottom of the stairs. He fell forward on the steps. His get-up-and-go had gotten up and left.

Misty Dawn nodded at Mary Jane who leaned down and grabbed him by the collar, lifting him up enough so he could see the bottom of Misty Dawn's feet. Had he even tried to head butt Mary Jane, she would have slammed him into the handrailing on the steps. Well, maybe she would have or maybe not. I was glad he decided not to do that so I wouldn't need to see any more blood in my pool.

"Let's try this again," began Misty Dawn in a conversational tone while she dipped her chip into the salsa. "Where is the guy you stuck in the hiney? More importantly, did you kill him?"

The guy shook his head no. "I put him in my trunk and gagged him."

Flo and Myrtle Sue went running out of the house.

"Mr. Smarty Pants, you better pray he's still alive and okay." She licked the salsa off her fingers followed by a swig of coke. "Who hired you to come out here to Parker's house? Before you tell me whoever it is who's going to kill you, depending on your answer, I'll let you go and that way you have a head start on whoever it is."

He nodded.

Misty Dawn put her hands up to her ear. "I can't hear you."

"I don't know the guy's name." He panicked when he saw Mary Jane pick up the volleyball again. "Wait, wait. I don't know his real name. I've seen him one time. He told me his name was Gus."

"Gus?" What kind of name is Gus?

"The deal was I was supposed to keep an eye on Parker and see what she was doing with the money."

"What money?" I was confused. I absolutely had zero anything to do with money. I had a budget for the tv show and my job was to stay within those numbers which I was doing.

"You know. The money you were supposed to get either tonight or tomorrow."

The girls and I all looked at each other totally mystified. I finally said, "Do y'all know anything about any money?"

They shook their heads no. Turning back to the guy, I asked, "What's your name?"

"Huh."

"What's your name?"

"It's, um, David."

"David, are you telling me I am supposed to have cash delivered to me here, at my house?"

He nodded yes.

"And all you're supposed to do is watch me and see where I'm going with it?"

Again, he nodded yes.

"You're not supposed to kill me or anything?" I was a little dubious as to the veracity of his comments. "How much money is it and, more importantly, how is it being delivered?"

"You're supposed to have three briefcases delivered to you."

"Three suitcases?" asked Rhonda Jean. I could see she was doing the fancy thumb dance on her phone. "Three million dollars?"

He looked at her. "I don't know."

"Three million dollars, Rhonda Jean? How do you figure that?" That was a serious amount of cash money.

"According to geekbeat.tv website, a million dollars in cash could fit in a deep briefcase and three briefcases means three million dollars." She looked up and smiled. "I'm assuming we're not investing the money in the Florida lottery."

I rolled my eyes. "No." Turning back to David, I said, "Why me? What am I supposed to be doing with this money?"

He shrugged.

Flo came jogging back into the house and said, "I've called 911. The guy is totally out. He was barely breathing, cold to the touch, and almost blue when we got to him. Myrtle Sue gave him mouth-to-mouth. He's breathing better but it's still iffy." She turned and jogged back out through the front door.

Mary Jane started bouncing the volleyball, hard. It was making a serious whack sound every time it bounced on the concrete. This was not a dainty method of dribbling a ball, it was an intense act of intimidation.

Misty Dawn glared at David. "He dies, you die. What you just went through in the pool won't even register on what we'll do to you."

David paled even more and he was shivering in the water.

"Mary Jane, go back out there with Flo and wait for the ambulance."

"Think I should stay here." Bouncing the ball harder.

"Go."

"One hit before I go."

"No. Go. Parker and I will take care of her, um, guest. I need you to be out there to make sure the rescue folks stay out of the house."

Mary Jane wasn't happy, but she left. I could only imagine what she was thinking.

Curiously, I looked at Misty Dawn and then said, "What are we going to do with him?"

"You've got gators back there on the riverbank, right?"

"Noooo," begged David. "Nooo, please don't feed me to the gators."

Suddenly, Misty Dawn held up her forefinger for all of us to be quiet. She cocked her head slightly to the side still listening intently.

"We've got company and I don't think it's who we want. Flip the lights, Parker."

Running into the kitchen, I found the panel and flipped the main switch to off. I had had the good sense to shut my eyes before turning off the power that way when I opened my eyes I could see in the dark.

Misty Dawn had come into the kitchen and thrust an AR-18 into my hands. She also put night goggles on me which I promptly re-adjusted so I could see.

"Landing party coming up from the river. They're probably going to get here just about the same time the fire rescue guys will."

"What did you do with the guy?"

"Don't worry about him, Parker. And, before you ask, no, he's not dead."

"Ladies," said a male voice behind me. A hand was clapped over my mouth and I was lifted up slightly before I could keel over from fright.

I screamed, no sound came out. I like to think I'm pretty calm and collected. Obviously not. It's amazing the lies we tell ourselves. My nerves were fried.

"Parker," in a whispered voice. "It's Denny. Be quiet."

I nodded my head up and down. I was grateful it was Denny and not some other whacko. He lowered me to the floor.

"Flo texted me," he explained. "I've got three guys out there now. They should be herding the intruders up here any minute now."

I could see flashing red and blue lights of the fire rescue guys bouncing around through the windows in front of my house.

Flo came running back into the house and up the stairs.

"She's back?"

I nodded although I didn't think he could see me. "Yes. Long story, tell you later but she can't be seen right now."

"Go out front and get them to take Jake to the ER ASAP, Parker."

Okay, I now knew the name of Denny's guy. I took off the night vision goggles handed them and the gun to Denny. Going out front, in addition to the fire rescue guys, I discovered the one and only Julian trying to ask the girls questions.

"My, my," I said sarcastically. "What brings you to my humble abode?"

"Radio dispatch told me a man was found in the trunk of a car. Sounds like a detective was needed on the scene." He sounded a little defensive. "Why aren't the lights on in your house?"

"Probably because it's close to dawn." I snorted.

"I have a lot of questions, like why is a guy in the trunk of a vehicle that isn't even registered to you?"

Oops. We hadn't had time to come up with a good story as to why Jake was in the trunk.

"Julian, do we really need to go over all of this right now? The only thing I can tell you is I don't know. I don't know who the car belongs to or anything else about it." Okay, that part was true. I didn't know who owned the car. "I do know the guy is a member of my security team." Again, that part was true.

"How did he come to be in the trunk and almost dead?"

"Julian," I was starting to get exasperated. Plus, I wanted to know what was going on in the back of my house. I was sure whoever it was approaching my house from the river was not inviting me to a social event. "Get Jake to tell you what happened, I simply don't know." Okay, that may have been a little white lie but my intentions were good...maybe.

He pointed his finger at me. "I'll be talking to you later."

Myrtle Sue and Mary Jane trudged up the steps past Julian. "Parker, you need to call the power company about how often it goes out."

"How's Jake?"

"Myrtle Sue brought him back to life, twice." Mary Jane wrapped her arm around Myrtle Sue's shoulders. "I think she's a hero."

"What were all of you gals out here for at this time in the early morning?" asked Julian. He had his little notepad out and writing in it.

"We're the Lady Gatorettes," snapped Mary Jane. "And we come and go as we want. What's it to you?"

All of our nerves were a little tight, to put it mildly. What Julian didn't know wouldn't hurt him. I'm sure they wanted to know what was going on with the lights off as well.

"Listen..."

"Julian, go home. None of us know anything and we're not going to know anything until we've gotten some sleep." I was tired. I hoped I managed to convey this to the nosey deputy.

With that, I walked up the steps and through my front door where I was greeted with both girls flattened against the wall.

"What's going on?" whispered Myrtle Sue.

"A landing party from the river. Denny's here and his guys are out back." I whispered back. "Misty Dawn was in the kitchen. I turned off the lights so it would be harder for them to see us."

"Not if they have night goggles," responded Mary Jane.

"Au contraire, oh wise one, they can't see through the glass in my house. Remember, I have those special wowy, zowy glass windows no one can see through with heat or night goggles. We can see out but they can't see us."

"Whatever. I'm assuming things are about to get exciting," she said drily. "Since I don't see any more flashing lights out there, I'm guessing Julian's gone. I don't see his cruiser. Where's Flo?"

"Upstairs."

"Let's go back into the kitchen and see what's happening," said Myrtle Sue.

"Myrtle Sue? Thanks for saving Jake."

"Sure."

We all made it back to the kitchen. The lights were still off. I could smell coffee and I'm guessing Denny made it. I don't think I've ever seen Misty Dawn make coffee. Getting doughnuts, yes; making coffee, no.

"Parker?"

"Yes, Denny, what's going on?"

"There's three of them and I have three of my guys out there. We should have company soon. Mind telling me what's going on?"

"Yoo hoo! Anybody down there?" From the sound of her voice, Flo was standing at the top of the stairs.

We all shushed her. Swift, silent, and deadly were part of the Lady Gatorettes' creed, or maybe it was just embedded in their DNA and they found each other by magic, but Flo was suddenly standing next to me.

"How do you do that?" I gasped, once again being startled to the point of almost screaming. The thought flitted through my mind that maybe I shouldn't be a Lady Gatorette because my nerves came unglued at the drop of a hat. If I was behind a computer working on a security breach, I was completely calm. I have nerves of steel. I've seen several of the girls behind the computer and although they're pretty tech savvy, they also get rattled very easily. Yes, they were wusses. In my mind anyway, I sure wasn't going to say that to them out loud.

"We're going to have to train you," giggled Flo. "But it'll have to be after this tv season is over."

Glad she was concerned about the shooting schedule. We only had four more shows to go. Hopefully, we could get them finished. I knew I did not want to be the director if there were a second season.

A couple of light taps on the sliding glass door to the kitchen could be heard. Denny opened the door, the lights came on, and there were three dog-ugly men who had been zip tied hands and feet with a gag in their mouths were laying in a bundle at the door. From their appearance, it looked like they had been dragged through the grass and probably not too gently either.

One of Denny's guys asked, "Do we need to stay?"

"By the boat. Let me know if anyone else comes up." Denny turned his attention to the men, nudging one of them with his military boot. "Gentlemen, what's it going to be, my way or the highway? Let me remind you, I'm standing over you and you're immobilized. What's it going to be?" He grinned with a wicked smile. Dare I say it looked deadly? I had not seen that smile in a really long time, I had shivers running up and down my spine.

I was pretty sure none of the girls had actually killed anyone, although I was quite convinced they could, and would, if provoked enough. However, I knew beyond the shadow of a doubt Denny had caused the demise of others. He had been in special ops in the military and I knew they didn't have their enemies sit down, play patty-cake, and have a tea party with them.

"Umph."

"Oh, yes, you're right. How can you possibly answer me with a gag in your mouth?" He leaned down and yanked it out. He looked expectantly at the man.

"We came to get the money."

Denny looked at me quizzically. "Parker, you holding out on us?"

I threw my hands up in the air. "Everybody listen up, I have absolutely no clue what money they're talking about. I don't do business this way, not in my company, not in my personal life."

Looking at the man, Denny hauled him up into a sitting position. "Tell me what you know."

The man started talking. I couldn't believe what a wimp he was. David held out longer than this guy did and that wasn't very long at all.

"She's supposed to get three million dollars delivered to her in three briefcases."

"Why and, more importantly, what is she supposed to be doing with them?"

"She's supposed to give them to Ryan Strickland..."

"Whoa!" I shouted. "He's dead, he was murdered."

"Maybe yes, maybe no." The guy had the audacity to actually smirk.

Mary Jane had picked up the volleyball and was starting to bounce it intently on the concrete. I groaned inwardly, hoping she wasn't going to smash this guy's face in. As close as she was to him, she could do some serious damage.

"Who was Danny Durham and why was he murdered?"

A thought occurred to me. I quickly texted Missy with my question.

The guy shrugged. The other two men were starting to wiggle around trying to sit up. Misty Dawn went over and yanked them both up to sitting positions.

"Can you guys talk or is it only Chatty Cathy here?" she asked.

They both kind of nodded at the other guy. She left their gags in. No point in having them talk then.

My phone pinged. I read the text and nudged Denny who read it. Missy was great at finding obscure information.

"Ryan had a brother named Arthur, right?"

The guy's eyes flickered for a moment. "Maybe, I don't know."

"He seriously ticked off someone, didn't he?"

The guy's eyes darted around as if they were a ball in a pinball machine.

I interrupted, "Arthur was Ryan's twin brother, wasn't he? He was the one who wanted to be a director, not Ryan."

The guy was bobbing his head up and down. His eyes wide. I wasn't sure if it was from fright or just that I had figured the connection out.

"Tell me about Arthur," I encouraged him.

"All I know is Ryan has, had, an identical twin brother who always wanted to be in the tv industry. He wasn't an actor, but he had a lot of chutzpah. He convinced people he could get tv shows on air."

Misty Dawn snapped her fingers. "Ryan's the one who figured out how to launder money through the tv shows."

"I guess. I know Arthur enjoyed being in the industry and going to different events, being a bigwig. Ryan's the smart one."

"He let his brother be murdered though," murmured Myrtle Sue.

The guy nodded again. "I don't know if he knew that was going to happen."

Rhonda Jean, our ever-lovable trick play master, was probably running different strategies through her brain. I saw her diagramming something on a piece of paper on my kitchen countertop. She looked up and around. "What? I'm figuring things out. I think some of this stuff is a diversion from what's really going on."

She had a point. I certainly didn't think this was a Point A to Point B type of thing. There were too many variables for it to be that. The more I thought about it, the more I was convinced whatever was going on was much bigger than what we initially thought.

"So, who are you working for?" Flo was smiling and batting her eyes at him.

"No!" we all shouted. Various chatter of "Not again, Flo!" "Stop it, Flo!" "You're kidding!" erupted from the girls.

"What?" she was trying to act innocent. "I might be able to get more info from him than y'all are but now that you've ruined it, you can just figure it out yourself." She stomped back upstairs.

Mary Jane hollered after her, "You stay in this house, missy, 'cas we're not tracking you down again and bringing you back to civilization!"

I heard a raspberry being blown from upstairs. We all looked at each other, rolled our eyes, and kind of laughed.

"Bad time of the month for her?" grinned Denny.

We all shrugged, that was one topic we didn't keep track of on each other.

"Women." The guy laughed. Mary Jane threw the volleyball and hit him smack on his forehead causing it to bounce on the sliding glass door several times. We all looked at her. A red welt immediately formed on the guy's forehead.

"Sorry, my arm twitched."

I could tell Denny was having a hard time not laughing. "You never answered the lady's question. Who are you working for?"

"Snake, and I don't know his real name." He was trying to focus his eyes. I strongly suspected he probably now had a concussion judging from the way he was blinking his eyes and his head rolling around a little.

"He texts me when he has a job, sends me the money electronically, I let him know when the job is finished, and he sends me the rest of the money."

Denny clicked on his radio. "Check the boat for a phone."

The answer came back almost immediately. "Negative."

"Which one of you girls wants to frisk this guy?" asked Denny, smiling. "Mary Jane, what about you?"

"No!" the guy shouted. "She'll hit me and I'll drown in the pool."

I started doing the Gator Chomp. "Gooo Gators!" The rest of the girls followed my lead. Mary Jane was dancing around making moves to grab him and the guy was trying to squirm away from her.

Of course she found his cell phone. It was in his front breast pocket. She handed it to Denny as she was dragging the guy over to the edge of the pool.

Yes, it was total meanness on my part but I kept up the Gator Chomp and the Go Gators chant as did the rest of the girls.

Mary Jane grabbed him by the front of his military shirt, lifted him up and tossed him into the pool. Man, she was strong! She had thrown him in the shallow end and he was trying to gain his balance to stand up.

"Oops, I did it again!" She laughed while continuing to dance.

"Britney Spears." Yes, I knew all of Britney's songs. I loved her music and her dancing.

We all laughed. The guy was still trying to figure out how to get out of the pool. Denny finally leaned over and dragged him up so he could lean back on the steps. He was huffing and spitting water out of his mouth.

"Are you trying to kill me?"

"Um, what were you going to do to Parker, humm? Turn about is fair play." Rhonda Jean laughed.

"That's different."

BAM! Mary Jane smacked the volleyball on top of his head.

She shrugged. "The water made the ball slippery."

None of us said anything, it was a whatever type of moment. Looking around, it suddenly dawned on me David wasn't out on the pool patio with us and I knew he wasn't in the kitchen.

"Where's David?"

"Oh, yeah. I almost forgot about him." Denny walked over to the pool bathroom and opened the door. Dragging him out to the rest of the guys, he nodded, "Do you know any of these guys?"

He looked at them and shook his head no.

Denny looked at the dazed guy in the pool. "Do you know him?"

The guy was barely coherent. Mary Jane's excellent ball handling skills had apparently rattled his brains. "N-n-no."

Myrtle Sue spoke up. "This is a burner phone and only has one phone number in it."

"What's the area code?" I asked. Not that it really made any difference, but I was curious as to a rough location.

"Chicago."

"Wasn't Ryan incarcerated near there?" I turned to look at David and the guy still in the water. He was making no effort to get out of the pool. Of course, with Mary Jane having little to no control over her throwing arm, I'd be a little reluctant to take a chance on her throwing another volleyball at my head also. She was not going to be pitching for any major or minor baseball team any time soon with her lack of accuracy. Yes, you can laugh because she's very accurate.

After questioning the guys for a few more minutes and determining they didn't really have much more information, Denny turned to me. "You want to let them go, Parker, or put them back in their boat and call that number in the phone?"

"We won't make it back to Jacksonville alive," whined David.

"Not really our problem is it...gator bait." Misty Dawn was letting her inner Marine out.

I was thinking furiously. I didn't want to be responsible for their deaths although they apparently thought nothing of bringing me to an early demise.

"You came down from Jacksonville, right?" They nodded their heads. "What if you continued south on the river to Dunns Creek and got one of your buddies to take you to Orlando? You could disappear from there."

They all looked at each other and kind of shrugged. They had the choice of maybe getting away from their current employer, doubtful but it could be done, or probably meeting an early death if they went back to Jacksonville.

David finally said, "Just let us take the boat and we'll disappear."

I nodded to Denny. "Give them a twenty-minute start and then I'll make the call."

"Thought you said you were going to give us thirty minutes," grumbled one of the guys as Denny was cutting the zip ties.

"Take it or leave it, dip weed."

Denny's men had come up from the boat and then escorted the soggy landing party back where they deposited them not very gently back into the boat.

"Y'all, we've been up all night. In fact, I think it's safe to say, most of us have been up thirty-six hours or more. The sky is waking up to a new day and all I want to do is go to sleep." We all looked like we had been rode hard and hung up wet. Our faces did not have the youthful glow we normally sported, all of our eyes were drooping, and we were moving a teensy, tiny bit slower than we usually did. "I'm going to bed and turning off my phone. Y'all are more than welcome to sleep here or go home but I'm going to bed. Last one out, set the alarm."

Mary Jane snatched the guy's phone that was laying on the countertop. "I need to make a phone call."

Myrtle Sue pointed out, "It hasn't been twenty minutes yet, Mary Jane."

"So what?"

I started to head up the stairs, but my curiosity overrode my fatigue.

Mary Jane punched the number in the phone. "Hey, want to let you know your guys failed. Now, is that anyway to talk to a lady?" Mary Jane was grinning. "Do you want to know what's happened to them or do you want me to hang up the phone on you, you piece of vermin? Yeah, well, no money's showed up. We know nothing about it, leave Parker alone, and your guys have gotten back into their boat and left about twenty minutes ago and, no, I don't have their itinerary." Laughing, she disconnected the phone. Almost immediately, it rang. None of us girls bothered to answer it. I guess it must have bothered Denny because he did hit the on button but didn't say anything. He had pushed the speaker button so we could all hear.

"This isn't over. We want our money back."

Denny disconnected the call. I was too tired to even care about any threats.

"By the way, Denny, where's Potus?" I was curious.

"Guarding my house out in the woods."

"Okay, just wanted to make sure he's safe. Good night, good morning, good whatever, I'm going to bed. Y'all know where everything is." I dragged my poor, tired body up the stairs.

CHAPTER 14

I woke up with the sun streaming in my bedroom. The delicious aroma of coffee was tickling my nostrils and beckoning me to the kitchen.

Once again, I discovered Myrtle Sue was already in the kitchen and whipping up another humongous breakfast. I don't believe the woman ever sleeps.

"Hey, Myrtle Sue, it sure smells good." I poured myself a cup of coffee.

"You didn't have any other food to cook other than breakfast," she grinned, "this will have to do."

The rest of the girls drifted into the kitchen, poured themselves a cup of coffee, and found seats either at the kitchen table or the countertop. Myrtle Sue dished the food on the plates and slid it over to them. Good thing she slid the food to them, otherwise, her fingers might have disappeared. They wolfed down the food and this was how I knew they were full, they picked up their plates, rinsed them off in the sink, and put them in the dishwasher.

I tapped my hand on the countertop. "Y'all, we need to have a quick meeting."

They all nodded while refilling their coffee cups. Flo brought me a fresh cup.

There was a knock at the front door. Bambi in the headlights could not have been more surprised. Since it was my house, it was up to me to answer the door. I hoped it was not Julian or some other deranged individual.

I looked at the door camera and grinned. Myrtle Sue was so thoughtful. She had ordered two dozen doughnuts and they guy had put them on the little table next to the door. I saw him driving off.

Knowing my life might not be as valuable as the doughnuts if I just brought them in, I yelled out to the girls. "Everyone, turn your back to the front door."

They all did that while I was running into the kitchen and flung the doughnut boxes on the countertop. I was not close enough to be run over. I never even got the word 'doughnuts' out of my mouth before they had all turned around and dive bombed the boxes.

"Thanks, Myrtle Sue, for ordering them." I had managed to grab a doughnut without losing my life or my fingers.

"We can't think without doughnuts," garbled Myrtle Sue and reaching for another one.

Swallowing the last bit of my glazed doughnut, I tapped on the countertop again. "Y'all, what are we missing on this Danny-Ryan thing? It's gotta be something obvious."

"I've been thinking about that," said Rhonda Jean, wiping her mouth and licking her fingers. "What if this whole thing has been a diversion?"

Nodding my head in agreement, "I think I need to make a couple of phone calls to see if the government is involved in this. It doesn't make sense that they charged and convicted this Ryan guy, put him in a federal prison, made big national news about it, and, for all intents and purposes, let him escape without ever saying anything about it. It simply does not make sense."

"Maybe he, Ryan, double-crossed everyone and the three million dollars is to help him start a new life," volunteered Flo as she was licking her fingers and reaching for another doughnut.

"Did the government know he has a twin brother?" asked Mary Jane. At least she was washing her hands from the doughnut sugar residue and not licking her fingers. "The real question is was Danny really Danny or was he really Ryan pretending to be Danny and got himself accidently killed?"

"Humm, that's a good point," I mused. "Who's the medical examiner here in River County?"

Misty Dawn spoke up first, "Jerry Banks. Let me call him."

"Oooo," all of the girls went at one time. I looked at them, puzzled. Obviously, I was missing something here. Had Misty Dawn cheated on John Boy with Jerry?

"Misty Dawn and Jerry had a thing going before she married John Boy," explained Mary Jane, winking at me. "He's always had a crush on her."

"Not a crush after all these years," opined Flo, "true love. Kind of like Parker and Joe D. He still loves you, Parker."

I flushed beet red. "Joe D. has nothing to do with this." I snapped my fingers. "Wait. I wonder if he knows anything about offshore money laundering?"

"Yes!" shouted the girls.

That was scary to know that they know he knows about that topic. Whew! What a mouthful!

"Do I dare ask how you know that?" I tried arching my eyebrow once again and failing miserably, once again.

"Because he actually taught a seminar on that in Orlando one time and it was in the paper," explained Misty Dawn grinning. "He told me later he had gotten a lot of new business here in Po'thole from that one article."

My eyebrows had raised my hairline by several inches I was sure. "What did he do? Take a course and now he's suddenly an expert?" Yes, I was being sarcastic.

"Hey, you talk loud enough and long enough, you get believers," shrugged Rhonda Jean and then admitted. "Big T and I gave Joe D. some money. I don't know exactly how he invested it, but I do know Big T and I are making money and that's all we really care about."

Misty Dawn and Myrtle Sue both nodded their heads. I'm assuming that meant they had also done the same thing.

"Before you ask, yes, John Boy and J.W. both knew we were investing with Joe D. Like Rhonda Jean said, we really only care about our money growing which it's doing at a much better rate than it is here in the U.S.," explained Myrtle Sue.

Who knew the girls were savvy investors? Yes, I also had invested money overseas but never with Joe D. Mainly because I knew that was opening up a whole new can of worms.

I strongly suspected if he had a clue as to how wealthy I really was maybe his love for me would turn into a major love for my money. Best to let things stay the way they were and most of my investments being handled out of Atlanta.

Mind you, I'm not saying Joe D. isn't trustworthy or even a good CPA. He is an excellent CPA. After all, he did name his firm We Make Money and he does. His clients are all very happy.

Maybe the reason why he knows so much about offshore banking and money laundering is because he's had so many wives and he wants to keep them from knowing how much money he really has. Divorce is very expensive.

"You need to call him, Parker," suggested Flo, blinking her eyes.

Snorting, I said, "Flo, you don't want to date or even marry Joe D."

"Why, Parker, what would make you think I'd want to do that? I could've married him years ago but he knows little to nothing about football or the Gators."

I laughed, "You must have had a date with him during football season and discovered that or you'd been married to him."

The rest of the girls laughed and nodded. Even Flo kind of grinned and nodded.

"Misty Dawn, call Jerry Banks and find out if he took a blood sample from Danny. See if he can run it through CODIS and get a hit as to who exactly it is who was murdered."

"Parker, what does CODIS mean?" asked Myrtle Sue. "I don't believe I know that acronym."

"It stands for Combined DNA Index System and it's maintained at the national, state, and local levels. Ask him to check at the national level. I doubt that Danny or Ryan is going to show up on the state level."

Misty Dawn was punching buttons in her phone. Since it was more than one button, I'm guessing Jerry Banks wasn't in her contact list.

Holding up her hand for all of us to be quiet, "Hey, Jerry, it's Misty Dawn. Yeah, I'm doing great. How you doing?" After getting all of the standard pleasantries out of the way and getting caught up on local gossip, she finally led into, "Could you do me a favor? You know the guy that was killed on our tv set? Yeah, well, who was he really?"

She suddenly stood up and started to pace in the kitchen. "Un, huh, yeah, okay, sure, um, thanks. Sorry you couldn't help me. You and Bobbi Diane need to come over some weekend and John Boy'll grill us up some steaks. Yeah, I can drop off seven chicks tomorrow. Your kids will love them. Yeah, you too, bye."

Misty Dawn laid her phone on the countertop, ran her hands through her hair, nodding her head up and down, and gazing without seeing in the kitchen.

Once she had stood up and was pacing the kitchen, I sensed something was seriously out of kilter.

"What's going on?" I asked, my voice low.

Misty Dawn snapped her fingers twice at Rhonda Jean who nodded. She left the kitchen for a few minutes. For once, the girls weren't chattering like monkeys in the South American rainforest. Flo tapped her lips looking at me.

Rhonda Jean popped back in the kitchen with a little key fob looking thing. Everyone put their phones on the counter. I did too although I wasn't one hundred percent sure what was going on.

She ran the key fob over each phone front and back, paused for about thirty seconds and then did the same thing again.

"None of us are bugged. It's got to be coming from his end," she announced.

"Tell us what Jerry said." Inquiring minds desperately needed to know.

"He said he couldn't talk about it. The FBI called and had him forward his findings to them. It is considered national security. Then the CIA showed up and took his samples, also saying it was national security related."

She took a gulp of probably now cold coffee. Continuing, she said, "He said everything was confidential."

"This is getting more and more interesting," I muttered.

"When we dated way back when, we had our own special code for not wanting people to listen in on our calls." She looked pointedly at the girls. They simply stared back at her although Flo almost snickered out loud.

"We also had our own way for when and where we were going to meet each other.

"He thinks his phones are tapped at the office." Looking around at the girls and me, she said, "I'm meeting him later. No one's going with me. Rhonda Jean, I've got a loose button on my Gator shirt. Do you have an extra one with you that can be sewed on?"

Whaat? Oh, yeah, mentally slapping myself in the head for not catching on immediately. She was putting a tracker on so if anything did happen to her, she could be located.

"I'll put it on for you and wrap it fifteen times since you always manage to tear the buttons off." Rhonda Jean was standing up and leaving the kitchen. "There's another clean shirt upstairs with a loose button, I'll put the new one on that shirt."

Really? How many sets of clothes do they have at my house? I really need to check those drawers.

"To have two different agencies call him and say it's national security related, that's just weird." I stated.

"Yes, it is. Parker, you know we need to do the show tomorrow, don't you?" asked Mary Jane.

Oops! I had almost forgotten about it. I was far more interested in this latest turn of events than I was in the tv show. However, people were on payroll, and I needed to get this show finished.

"I'm thinking we need to get Big T and Gator Tom together so they can say how Flo was rescued and Gator Tom can sell his mosquito potion to our viewers. What do you think?" asked Mary Jane.

"Misty Dawn, think you'll be back in time?" I asked.

She shrugged. "If I'm not, just say I ate too many doughnuts and had the terrible bad belly or turkey trots. Everyone will know what that means."

I cringed. These girls. But, she was right, the whole world would know what was wrong with her. Not sure if I'd do that on national tv but this was their show and I hesitated to mess with the success they were having.

"Misty Dawn, are you meeting Jerry tonight? It's already six and..."

"He goes for dinner around seven. Once Rhonda Jean finishes my shirt, I'm leaving. I'll let you know what's going on later."

CHAPTER 15

Everyone was still at my house at seven. We had ordered out for pizza. The thought occurred to me I should probably just buy the pizza place we always ordered from and that would save us money but, then again, we were helping to support the local economy.

All of a sudden, we heard Misty Dawn's voice come in loud and clear on the small receiving unit Rhonda Jean had placed on the patio table. How much stuff did they have at my house?!

"That's the button transmitter," explained Myrtle Sue, finishing up her last slice of pepperoni pizza. "Rhonda Jean set it up for fifteen miles."

Aha! That's what the wrapping it fifteen times meant. I'm assuming the code language was on the off chance someone somehow was listening in on our conversation.

"Jerry, good to see you." They exchanged the normal pleasantries from not seeing each other for several years.

"Okay, Misty Dawn, we can stop here." Jerry's voice sounded like he was in the same room with us.

Rhonda Jean whispered, "They're on the bleachers at the baseball field."

Flo giggled. "I've kissed many boys...and men, under those bleachers."

Mary Jane snorted. "We all have, it's a small town and our selection of men is limited."

I rolled my eyes and refused to acknowledge their male bragging prowess. I had kissed several boys under the bleachers as well while I was in high school, but I certainly wasn't going to admit to it.

With the exception of Joe D., none of the boys still lived around here and I wasn't going to give the girls ammunition for going on an internet scavenger hunt to find them. I knew if Mary Jane found any of them, she'd try to hook us up and I didn't want that.

Tapping her fingers on the table, Rhonda Jean was trying to get everyone to be quiet.

"Jerry, tell me what's going on? What's the big secret about Danny and his blood?" Misty Dawn was wasting no time in getting right to the point. She and I were bonded sisters on that skill set.

"What do you know?"

Apparently they were both looking around because Misty Dawn said, "I don't see anyone, do you?"

Jerry must have shaken his head no because Misty Dawn started. "Initially we thought Danny was Ryan Strickland and was hiding in plain sight as a tv director. Then we discovered Ryan had a twin brother named Arthur.

"Arthur was the one who wanted to be a tv director."

"Yes," interrupted Jerry. "I looked up this guy Danny Durham on the internet and he's been doing various tv shows for a couple of years. The show you Lady Gatorettes are on is the only show that's ever made it to tv. Everything else just washed out."

"Ah ha!" escaped from my lips. Everybody shushed me. I ignored them. "This whole thing..."

They all glared at me and me being the sometimes wimp that I am, I wilted. I pointed back at the receiver.

Jerry continued, "The body came in as Danny Durham. When I ran the blood sample through the CODIS, which is standard procedure by the way, it came back as classified."

Whoa! We were now receiving confirmation that something wasn't right.

"I've had classified cases before, and it's rare to have one here in Po'thole but it does happen. Anyway, I received my first phone call within forty-five minutes. I was told it was a matter of national security and just to identify the body as Danny Durham."

Something else was going on because we could hear them walking quickly.

"Jerry, what's really going on?" whispered Misty Dawn.

"Don't know. Here we need to get up this tree."

We could hear them climbing and then quiet. Well, except for an alarm that went off on Rhonda Jean's receiver. We all jumped.

Flo and Mary Jane ran out of the house. Hearing Flo's truck starting up and rumbling down my driveway, I was curious. "What's going on? Why are they climbing trees?"

"There may be a possible security issue for them. Misty Dawn's letting us know she may need backup."

"Should I get hold of Denny?"

"Nope, Flo and Mary Jane can handle it." She paused for a moment, "If we get two beeps, we all need to go."

"What happens with three beeps?"

"You don't want to know, Parker, you don't want to know."

"Do I dare ask how many beeps you guys ever needed on me?"

She laughed, "Just one, Parker. Misty Dawn's a totally different level than you."

That made sense and considering all of the crazy things that have happened to me over the past couple of years in this little town, I didn't want to be at the same threat level as Misty Dawn. My level was high enough for me.

Misty Dawn and Jerry were still silent although I could sort of, maybe hear some voices but couldn't make out what they were saying.

Rhonda Jean was fiddling with the receiver's knobs and the voices became very loud.

"Where'd they go?"

"Eliminate both of them?"

"Yes."

I looked at Rhonda Jean with my eyes wide and whispered, "Is this a level two or a level three?"

She shook her head no and held up one finger. She was intently listening.

"Can Mary Jane and Flo hear what's going on?"

Myrtle Sue answered, "Yes. More coffee, Parker?"

I needed more coffee like I needed a hole in the head, don't go there! But because I didn't want to be rude, I accepted it.

Then voices, voices we all knew and loved.

"I'm telling you I saw a buck out here."

"Don't believe you."

Yes, it was Mary Jane and Flo bickering not too far from the male voices cogitating on the demise of Misty Dawn and Jerry. Which also meant they were probably also directly under where Misty Dawn and Jerry were sitting in the tree.

One of the guys snarled, "What are you two bimbos doing out here?"

"Really? You own this property?" Flo was using her flirtatious voice. "I happen to know the county owns this ballfield and deer do happen to come to the edge of the woods around it. I saw a big three-pointer out here the other day and I wanted to find him again."

"You need to go on. This is official business," said one of the guys in an official sounding tone.

"Let me see your badge," demanded Mary Jane. I could almost hear her laughing.

"I just told you this is official business. You need to leave," snapped the guy.

"You're not local. I know most of the state guys and all of the local guys and the fact that you're not showing me your badge means you're full of crap. YOU go take a hike." Mary Jane was not backing down. "We have the right to be here and take as much time as we want. We plan to be here for a while."

"I said...yeah, yeah, okay, we're leaving now."

"You need to totally vacate this area now. We saw your car over there and it had better be gone in the next five minutes." Flo no longer was using her cutesy-cute voice. "Or little Oscar is going to dispose some nasty ammo into your legs and you'll have to drag yourself back to your car...assuming you can make it far before the dogs get you."

Little Oscar? I knew she carried a .380 ACP Smith & Wesson and I am assuming that's what she called it. Who names their handguns?

A few moments went by as Flo and Mary Jane were humming the song 'Bye Bye Bye' by NSYNC, then we heard, "Time for us to go home, our work is done."

Misty Dawn's voice came through so loud that Rhonda Jean and I clapped our hands over our ears as she quickly toned the sound down on the receiver.

"Thanks! Later."

Myrtle Sue's phone pinged. "They said they're on the way back."

We heard Misty Dawn and Jerry scrambling down from the tree.

"Here's the crazy thing, Misty Dawn, the call I received saying it was national security, I don't think it was. Maybe on the classification part but not on the phone call and not that quick, then to get another phone call fifteen minutes after that one saying it was the CIA and it was also national security. None of that makes any sense.

"I called a buddy of mine in the Orlando FBI office and asked him to take a look. He called me back a couple of hours later and told me to drop it, no more questions."

"Did you ask him why?"

"Yes, and he said no more questions, to just accept it as national security, and let it go."

"I'm betting you didn't."

Jerry agreed. "About an hour later, I did receive an email with a masked address..."

"Your buddy in the Orlando office."

"Yes. The email said Danny Durham was Arthur Strickland. Because the DNA was so close, they thought at first it was Ryan who had swapped places with Arthur and was murdered. Ryan had assisted the FBI in a sting operation on the money laundering group he was in."

"So, that means Ryan is still alive and the FBI doesn't know where he is."

"That's my guess and that's also why, I'm guessing, they don't want me to pursue this any further. Whoever murdered Arthur probably thought it was Ryan and..."

"They killed the wrong guy," finished Misty Dawn. "Which also means they didn't know Ryan had a twin brother. Ryan could be free from his money laundering guys knowing where he is and also the FBI."

"Yes. Misty Dawn, I need to get back to the office."

"Gotcha. Okay, I'll let you know what we find out. Be safe."

Famous last words.

CHAPTER 16

Wow! Talk about a double cross! How did the bozos who came up the river to my house know that Ryan and Arthur were twins? Still a lot of unanswered questions.

I'm guessing the three million dollars that is supposed to be delivered to me is for Ryan and he's going to disappear. I am really hoping he has zero desire to do harm to me...or to make me disappear, permanently. I'm hoping he's just going to take the money and run.

Once we all convened again in my kitchen and were chowing down on, what else, pizza, Misty Dawn said, "Think we should catch him, Parker, or just let it all go?"

I almost choked. Misty Dawn asking for my opinion on something? I was moving up in the world. Swallowing, I answered, "I think we should focus on the tv show. If anyone is watching me, us, I want them to think everything is normal and we don't know, don't care, not interested in anything else."

They all nodded their heads.

"We need to do the show tomorrow morning. Do we have a plan on what we're doing?" Looking around, I questioned them. "I'm assuming y'all are going to let the world know that Flo has been saved by Big T and Gator Tom?"

Flo waved her hands. "I should be the one to thank Gator Tom for his hospitality."

"You're hoping he's not going to kidnap you," laughed Rhonda Jean. "I'm not swimming through that nasty muck again to save you."

"If it happens again, you're on your own," agreed Mary Jane.

"Flo," a very stern look from Misty Dawn, "this isn't happening again. Do you understand?"

Flo smiled and waved her hands. "Yep."

"Do you have a way for getting in touch with Gator Tom so you can let him know that tons of people are going to want to buy his bug spray?" I was curious.

"Oh, yes, that girl Skye Taylor is going to go out there."

We all groaned.

"No, no. Gator Tom told me he comes into town once a week to get some groceries. Skye's going to wait for him at the store and then tell him what's going on..."

"Big T is going to be there also," interrupted Rhonda Jean. "He's going to cooperate with Gator Tom on this."

"Okay, ladies, here's what's going to happen when you announce Flo has been saved." I proceeded to give them advanced warning on what the national media was probably going to do. Yes, Flo was probably going to be a big star...at least for her fifteen minutes of fame.

The girls all agreed, well Flo didn't but whatever, they would keep Flo from getting married until football season started. The possibilities of men swarming all over her once she was on the national news was high.

Flo was cute after all. Much as I hated to admit it, my skill set in this area being severely lacking, Flo attracted men like bees to honey.

Why? We all knew she wouldn't marry anyone during Gator football season. It was highly doubtful that any potential suitor would be allowed to watch Gator football with the girls. If he did, and he survived an entire season with the girls, he might be considered a possibility for Flo; however, since none of their husbands watched any of the games with them, it was highly doubtful any other sane male could make it. That alone would make a marriage prospect highly suspect. It was a darned if you do and darned if you don't scenario.

My phone went off. Glancing at the caller ID, I groaned.

The girls all clapped their hands, hooted, hollered, and laughed at my discomfort.

"I'm not answering it."

More hoots and hollers.

"Seriously, Saffron can wait until we get the tv show straightened out..."

"And those little nasty murders," giggled Flo.

"You keep getting best-selling books when you are around us." Rhonda Jean laughed, "You might want to talk to your book agent every time she calls."

Shaking my head, I pushed the on button. "Saffron, I'm really busy right now but I'll call you in two days." I hung up. The phone rang again and the girls were still doing their catcalls and laughing. I ignored the phone because it was Saffron calling me back.

As everyone left to go home, I hoped Skye wouldn't be kidnapped by Gator Tom at the store tomorrow.

CHAPTER 17

"Five, four, three, two, one, and you're live!"

"Helloooo, viewers! Do we have some good news for you or what!" Misty Dawn was bouncing up and down behind the microphone. "We have..."

"I'mmm back!" shouted Flo, grinning from ear to ear. "Y'all are just not going to believe what happened to me!"

"Tell me more, tell me more. Was it love at first sight?" sang Rhonda Jean, Mary Jane, and Myrtle Sue. They knew all the words to all of the songs in the movie Grease.

"Take it away, Flo!" shouted Misty Dawn.

"Well, y'all know, we received a lovely fan letter from Gator Tom..."

"Tell me more, tell me more." The rest of the girls were still singing and Misty Dawn had joined in with them. They actually had really nice voices.

The errant thought popped in my mind that maybe, just maybe, with the right encouragement, I could get them a record deal and they could go on the road touring. What a blast we would have!

I could set up another company to promote them...and that's when I realized I had probably consumed way too much sugar this morning. I don't need any new projects. BUT, it was a thought.

"I was wandering around out in the Ocala National Forest, got lost, and was eaten up alive by our killer Florida mosquitoes. Gator Tom found me, put some of his wonderful bug spray on me, and then took me to his little cabin.

"By the next morning, I didn't have any mosquito bites on me." She was breathless.

"No mosquito bites at all?" asked Mary Jane grinning.

"No! They were all gone. I couldn't believe it." Flo paused for a moment. "If y'all want any of this magic bug spray, you can find it on our website."

"Tell the rest of the story," urged Myrtle Sue.

"Oh, yeah, well, Big T, Rhonda Jean's husband, was so concerned about me that he contacted Gator Tom and told him to be on the lookout for me."

I wondered how much effort Rhonda Jean expended in getting her husband to meet up with Gator Tom this morning. Hopefully, they wouldn't kill each other in the store.

"Anyway," Flo continued, "they both brought me back to civilization and life is good."

She was positively beaming. I could see the call-in board was positively exploding with little red dots indicating new calls were pouring in.

Mary Jane, Myrtle Sue, Rhonda Jean, and Misty Dawn were continuing to sing songs from Grease in the background. Flo was chattering away nine ways to Sunday to the viewing audience.

"Everyone, y'all need to get Gator Tom's bug spray. Check out our website. Till next time 'Go Gators!'" and the show was over.

Whew! That was a high octane show if there ever was one. We were all happy. Well, we were until Julian showed up.

"Well, Mr. Deputy, what can we do for you?" quizzed Flo. She still was on an adrenaline high from the show.

Julian walked straight up to me. He encroached on my personal space so I backed up.

"Why didn't anyone bother to let the Sheriff's office know that Flo was found? We spent man hours looking for her. You guys could have told us without my having to find it out on your show." He was fuming.

"Prove it." Misty Dawn was glaring at him.

"Prove what?" Julian was confused.

"Prove that you spent hours and hours looking for Flo because I don't believe you."

Fighting words for sure.

"How you coming on finding out who murdered Danny and Ronnie?" Myrtle Sue had a snarky smile plastered on her face.

Julian glared back at the girls and then turned to me. "The FBI is now involved and is handling everything. I expect them to come arrest you people at any time." And with that he stomped off.

Misty Dawn shouted at his back. "Go Gators!"

I couldn't help myself, I laughed out loud. So did the other girls.

I walked back to my tent where some of the crew had gathered so we could finish up details on the show. One of the camera guys said, "Oh, Parker, there was a delivery for you. I had them put it right there by your chair."

Curious, I walked around the table and there were three brown executive briefcases. How had this happened with so much security? How did the briefcases get delivered to me without anyone noticing? I darn sure wasn't going to open up the briefcases in front of everyone. Three million dollars would be enough enticement to have almost anyone kill me right there.

Scorpion was still guarding me. He eyed the briefcases when I turned to look at him. "I've been with you the entire time. No clue."

Waving at the camera guy, "How were the briefcases delivered or do you know?"

"I was coming in this morning and there was a delivery truck that had pulled up behind me. He came over and asked if I were going in. I said yes and he told me the briefcases were for you and where should he put them. So I brought him back here."

"Great, thanks." I texted Denny to take a look at the security cameras and see if he could determine who it was who delivered the cases.

We finished up the details on the show and left. I headed home with the briefcases. Seriously, did you really think I was going to leave them on the set?

Once I got home, Denny was already there along with the Lady Gatorettes.

"It looks almost like a UPS truck but it's not." Denny jumped right in there with the information. "The guy keeps his head down almost the entire time from leaving his truck to actually placing the briefcases in your tent. Every time he turned around he held his clipboard up to his face so we couldn't get a clear shot of it. He knew where the cameras were."

"So, no clue?"

"Nope."

"Parker," said Misty Dawn. "That Ryan guy is probably going to be showing up soon. Let's capture him."

Thinking for a moment, I said, "You know, as much as I would like to do that, I'm thinking if his old gang doesn't know he's alive and the FBI can't find him, let me just wish him well and send him on his way with the money."

Denny nodded in agreement.

Misty Dawn received a phone call. We all looked at her when it went off because she never received phone calls, texts, yes but calls almost never.

"Hello." She nodded her head a couple of times, cleared her throat, and said, "Yeah, okay, bye."

"What happened, Misty Dawn? Is John Boy okay?" asked Myrtle Sue hesitantly. The girls were all concerned.

"Yeah, he's okay. Jerry's been in a really bad accident and it's dicey if he's going to live or not."

"Oh, my goodness!" "No!" "What can we do?"

Misty Dawn shook her head, then muttered, "I wonder if it was truly an accident?"

Denny and I looked at each other, both of us thinking the same thing. It was probably not an accident. The new question became was Misty Dawn in any danger?

"None of you ladies are to be alone at any time until all of this is resolved," ordered Denny. "If you need security..."

They all snorted.

"Okay, whatever, but if you can't see other, then you need to check in every ten minutes or so by text."

"Denny, we have our plans already in place." Misty Dawn, ever the leader, took over. "We're good."

Nodding, he graciously stopped talking because he knew when he wasn't going to win.

I asked Misty Dawn, "Are you going to see Jerry in the hospital?"

She shook her head. "Nope, we're going to go look at his car and see if it's been messed with to cause his accident. Something's still not making sense about the FBI."

Denny was furiously texting someone on his phone and appeared to be ignoring us. I knew he was very much paying attention to what we were saying.

The girls all left, leaving just me and Denny. "So, what's going on, dude?"

"She's right, the FBI doesn't do a lot of the things that keep happening unless..."

I finished his thought. "Unless they've been turned. Denny, maybe Ryan's smarter than what everybody's been giving him credit for.

"We know he has to be very smart to begin with because he's managed to outwit the FBI and the money laundering group at every turn. To me, it means he's been planning this for quite some time."

"It's his backup plan, Parker. It's a piece of cake to do six months in a federal prison and then to be able to walk out of it without anyone noticing for hours."

"Well, remember, the wife of one of the guards is making an extra however many thousands of dollars a month.

"Denny, you just can't make me believe the FBI didn't catch onto that. Those guys are usually on top of things."

Snapping my fingers, I said, "Who's the FBI agent in charge? He's the one who is diverting all of the attention. He's the distraction factor."

Denny looked at me for a long moment. "I think Ryan has double-crossed everyone. The three million dollars is for him to completely disappear. I'm betting the money is going to be washed in some form or fashion out of the country and he's probably going to live out the rest of his life having fun. The FBI isn't going to spend a lot of time and money tracking him down.

"After all, he can't be tried again for the same crime, double jeopardy and all that. The CIA might go after him but probably not."

"Probably so, Denny, but what about the FBI guy he's screwed over?"

"Pure speculation, Parker, if that's what happened. Plus, the guy can only do so much before supervisors start noticing inconsistencies in his work life. If he suddenly took off and left the country, then he'll be watched for quite a while.

"If the money laundering guys think he has their three million dollars, they very definitely will send someone out to get him." Denny cleared his throat, "And to get their money back, whatever it takes."

We looked at each other thinking of the various scenarios that could occur yet knowing it could be something totally off the wall we hadn't thought of.

'So What' started playing on my phone. It was a number I didn't recognize. Okay, so I don't recognize most phone numbers calling me. Whatever. I will almost always answer the phone however.

"Parker Bell."

"Yes." It seems like I might have heard this voice before, but I wasn't sure. A lot of people sound similar on a phone.

"I believe you have something of mine."

I waved my hand at Denny and turned on the speaker phone.

"Maybe. What is it that I'm supposed to have?" If I were Flo, I could sound coquettish. But since I'm not, my question came out sounding flat.

The caller chuckled, "Three brown executive briefcases were delivered to you and you took them home with you."

It didn't occur to me until right then that he had probably enabled some type of tracking device on them. Made sense. It's something I would have done. Three million dollars is a lot of money...money I would certainly hate to lose.

"Parker, here's what I would like you to do. I want you to take the briefcases to the ballfield and place them under the bleachers behind home plate. Take your bodyguard guy with you if you wish. Then leave."

"Wait!" I almost shouted. "Then what? Are you going to shoot us in the back?"

He chuckled. "No, my dear. I personally don't shoot and kill people. Others do that.

"You and your gentleman friend can walk away and pretend none of this ever happened."

Denny was texting like a demon on hot coals. He shook his head at me.

"Ryan," I said, not sure how he was going to react to his name. "Tell me how all of this went down. I know you pretty much have to be a genius to come up with this plan."

Denny gave me a thumbs up. I was hoping a little flattery would work on Ryan.

He chuckled again. "Meet me in an hour." He disconnected.

Denny and I looked at each other. "I could get the Lady Gatorettes to surround the place and we could capture him."

He grinned. "Why? Who would we turn him in to? Remember, he's dead as far as anyone is concerned. Unless, of course, you're thinking about hiring him."

We both burst out laughing. I didn't want to admit to Denny that thought had actually crossed my mind. Hey, a girl can always use a new way not to pay taxes...right? Let me point out, I do pay a lot in taxes and I'm happy to pay them because the United States is still the best country in the world to live in as far as I was concerned.

As we were loading the briefcases in the car, I heard Denny say softly, "We're not putting any tracking devices on these. Ryan can take them and do whatever he wants."

He pointed at his ear. Duh huh! Just slap me and call me Sally. We had had the briefcases in the house and Ryan had probably heard everything we had been talking about. Which, of course, made me curious as to how close we were to the actual truth of what had happened. We might never know. Being a nosy Nancy, I wanted to know everything.

We arrived at the baseball field and didn't see anyone. Denny didn't take out his binoculars, he hadn't contacted any of his guys We just simply put the briefcases under the bleachers and left.

***

Several weeks went by. The Lady Gatorettes were doing phenomenally well in the ratings on their reality show. We had a big party at the end, a wrap as it is called in showbiz. They were up for an Emmy for best reality show. I shuddered to think what could happen at the award show.

They had been asked to sing the Star-Spangled Banner at the first University of Florida Gator home football game. Others thought they could sing too, thus validating my original premise they could be singers. This was the highlight of the year for the Lady Gatorettes to be chosen to sing at The Swamp with their beloved Gator football team. No doubt in my mind that at the end of the song they would shout 'Go Gators!'

Gator Tom sold a ton of his mosquito bug spray and sold the company to a large conglomerate. He was smarter than what his appearance would indicate because he was also going to receive a hefty royalty on every bottle sold in perpetuity. Oh, yes, Flo did go out on a date with him to a fish camp where they both decided they'd like to remain friends but weren't going to date each other.

He and Big T still don't like each other, and trash talk each other at every opportunity they get. They just don't do it on national tv, social media, or to reporters.

Jerry was still healing and the girls did confirm the accelerator had been tampered with but couldn't prove who might have done it.

Deputy, detective, or whatever he's known as officially, Julian decided there wasn't enough evidence to convict any of us of murdering Danny or Ronnie. Of course, it helped tremendously that Robert explained the facts of life in a courtroom to him. Plus, I have it on good authority that the Lady Gatorettes might have *really* explained the facts of life to him regarding pursuing criminal charges against another Lady Gatorette.

Joe D. called me one day out of the clear blue sky and asked me to lunch. I was skeptical but he assured me he was still happily married, although he loved me the most out of any of his wives.

I met him at a local diner where the food had been passable the last time I ate there but they had new owners so I was hopeful the food had improved.

Joe D. was a very casual type of CPA. He strolled in wearing white jean shorts, a flowered shirt, and flip flops. It's Florida.

He kissed me on both cheeks as a greeting. Sitting down, we caught up on the local gossip and ordered our food.

"Parker, I have something for you."

"Joe D., I've told you a hundred million times I'm not going to marry you and we're not doing friends with benefits." I was not irritated or even annoyed. He and I went through this routine every time we saw each other. It was kind of an inside joke with us.

"Nope, nothing like that Parker. Here." He handed me a sealed manila envelope with just my name on it.

"What's in it, Joe D.? Am I being sued or something?" I turned it over to undo the clasp on the back and pulled out several sheets of typed paper.

"No. I was just told to give you this." He sat back smiling.

I looked up. "Do you know what it is?"

"Not exactly."

Our food arrived as I started to read. Now normally I have a very hefty appetite; however, I was more interested in the papers.

I read through it quickly, inserted it back into the manila envelope, and started to eat my lunch. "Joe D., you really don't know what was in the envelope?"

He smiled and shook his head. "No, I really don't and I'm pretty sure it's none of my business anyway."

I'll say this about Joe D., he always was and still is very discreet but, then again, being a CPA I expect he would need to be.

"Let me just ask you one thing."

"Sure."

"Do you or did you know a Ryan Strickland?" I was chewing around my food to ask the question.

"Sure." He smiled.

"How?"

"Oh, didn't I tell you? Ryan was the guy who taught me how to move money offshore for my clients. He's the guru of..."

"Money laundering," I finished his sentence.

"Well, I wouldn't say that exactly." He chewed for a moment. "I'll just say he's extremely creative and is a genius when it comes to moving money offshore."

I started to snicker. Joe D.'s mouth crinkled up into a smile and his eyes twinkled.

"Let me guess, you were his prize student and you guys became friends."

Joe D.'s smile became bigger and he wiggled his eyebrows.

We finished lunch and I headed back to my house. Denny was already there waiting on me. Yes, I had texted him.

He handed me a delicious cup of the brown nectar that kept my life going. I handed him the manila envelope grinning.

"It's just so satisfying to know that we were right about so many things on Ryan Strickland. Read it."

Denny looked at me and pulled the papers out of the manila envelope.

Parker, I enjoyed doing business with you. It was a delight to find someone who would actually follow my instructions.

You had questions. Arthur was my identical twin brother as you have found out. Everyone thought he was me and vice versa but, no, we were two separate people.

After I turned evidence over to the FBI, it was a very careless mistake on my part and one that will never happen again, and spent six months at the federal prison, my Chicago associates discovered there was three million dollars that the FBI had not accounted for in their indictment of me.

Of course, they were curious as to where the money was. Let me say that this was hard money and not digital numbers floating across a computer screen.

They paid off a guard's wife so I could simply walk off the campus and into a waiting car. Sad to say, but the driver suffered an unfortunate accident and is no longer in the land of the living.

My brother was getting ready to start filming that tv show with those crazy women you hang around with. I will say, they do have a certain flair for the inane and I do laugh at their antics.

My former Chicago associates discovered poor Arthur was directing the show and thought it was me. Because Arthur didn't know anything, he couldn't tell them anything. Unfortunately, they did not believe him and he passed away far too soon.

Ronnie happened to walk in right after Arthur was murdered. Chicago thought he had seen what had happened, he hadn't, and they decided it was best if he joined Arthur in eternity.

You're probably wondering about the money. I had put it in a storage locker thinking as soon as that silly show was over Arthur and I would go to the Bahamas and live out the rest of our days on the beach. I'll have a drink for Arthur on the beach every day for the rest of my life. He paid the ultimate sacrifice.

I knew who you were because of your cyber security business. You had actually stopped one of our offshore transactions for a particular government agency but had never turned us into the government. I knew you could be trusted. You have a great reputation in the industry.

I'm actually the one who delivered the briefcases to your tent. It was just so much safer that way.

Wondering about the FBI? You should. John Stoles was the agent I had dealt with initially. Long story short, he wanted half of the three million dollars as his 'fee' for misdirecting the agency on a number of things. Ain't happening. You might want to turn him in. He's been skimming money for awhile from various arrests. He has a woman problem.

So, once again, it was a pleasure picking up my money from you. I won't be coming back to the United States and I plan on living the rest of my life where it's warm and there are beautiful beaches as well as beautiful women.

As to my Chicago associates, let's just say they have their money and won't be looking for me anymore. They are also not interested in you or the Lady Gatorettes. You're safe.

The last remaining question you probably have is, was Joe D. in on all of this? The answer is no. Although I will say if you need money moved offshore, Joe D. was an outstanding student and has many satisfied clients.

Ryan

"Wow!" said Denny. "We were on the money for most of this."

Smiling, I nodded. "Life is good."

ACKNOWLEDGMENTS

T hank you to my wonderful support team for your encouragement, words of reassurance, and belief in me on those days when the blank computer screen would stare back at me like a one-eyed monster daring me not to write anything. I survived and conquered.

My wonderful team: Cindy Grooms Marvin, Nancy Haddock, Barb Smothers, Skye Taylor, Julie Zommers, Cathy Spence, Tommy Taylor, and Jordan Easton.

Thank you to my beta readers. As always, any errors are my full responsibility.

Thank you to all my loyal readers and fans. I greatly appreciate you!

ABOUT THE AUTHOR

Okay, true confession time. I have a wicked sense of humor in case you hadn't noticed. My true desire and hope is that I made you laugh while reading this book.

Break the stress factor in your life for just a few minutes every day and do something that you enjoy doing that is just for yourself.

I absolutely love readers because without you I'd be eating peanut butter and crackers. I greatly appreciate you and your support. The best reward I get is when someone tells me they laughed out loud at my books and that it brightened their day.

People are always asking if I'm available for speaking engagements. The short answer is "Yes, of course." In fact, I can even do a Facebook Live Video event for your readers group.

Be sure to go to my website AuthorSharonBuck.com, sign up for the newsletter, and receive a free book!

Thank you for being a loyal fan.

OTHER BOOKS BY SHARON E. BUCK

Parker Bell Florida Humorous Mystery Series

A Dose of Nice

A Honky Tonk Night

The Fabergé Easter Egg

Little Candy Hearts

Milton Keynes UK
Ingram Content Group UK Ltd.
UKHW020921181223
434584UK00001BA/245